The Wine Cellar

The Wine Cellar

Short fiction by
EDWARD BONETTI

THE VIKING PRESS  NEW YORK

Copyright © Edward Bonetti, 1971, 1972, 1974, 1977

First published in 1977 by The Viking Press
625 Madison Avenue, New York, N.Y. 10022

Published simultaneously in Canada by
Penguin Books Canada Limited

LIBRARY OF CONGRESS CATALOGING IN PUBLICATION DATA
Bonetti, Edward.
The wine cellar.
CONTENTS: Calder.—A case in point.—Fever.—
Beginner's luck.—Kopect's story.—The wine cellar.
I. Title.
PZ4.B7123wi [PS3552.O634] 813'.5'4 76-53794
ISBN 0-670-77210-0

Printed in the United States of America
Set in VIP Caledonia

"Calder" originally appeared in New Letters, Vol. 40 No. 2;
"Fever" in New American Review, No. 13;
"Kopect's Story" in The Harrison Street Review.

ACKNOWLEDGMENTS

Acknowledgments are rightly due to Ted Solotaroff for choosing the title "Fever," and to Gordon Lish, for his editorial insights concerning the story "Calder." I am especially grateful to Norman Mailer for his generous interest in all of these stories, and to Richard Goodwin, whose dogged will to see them in book form was the hammer that helped drive the nail home.

CONTENTS

The Wine Cellar

Calder

The dwellings that stood close to the road were rafters now, charred, armlike studs and beams. The hills he could see were marked by broken trees and rubble and a few tanks gone to rust. While he looked at this from beneath the canopy of the truck, he thought of his quarters back at the supply depot—some seventy miles to the rear of the convoy—and of his privacy there. He had been a noncombatant until the alert.

Warrant Officer, Raymond Calder, of Fifth Battalion's Quartermaster Corp, Twelfth Army Regiment, supervised the dispatching of supplies. His subordinates did the detailed work while he checked out their papers. The operation was efficient and complete, powered by something outside of his presence as the officer in charge, and not once that he could remember had he ever had to issue a direct order, or call a man down for his work. Because of this he felt no authority and he often wondered whether his men regarded him as their superior. If they don't, he resolved finally, it's nothing that matters to me.

He was in his late thirties. He had an unassertive nature and rarely spoke. He was intimate with no one and fell easily into periods of daydreaming while he sat at his desk at one end of the storage shed, usually staring at paper forms. He was a career man, a noncommissioned officer whose private quarters were located in a one-story wooden structure built during a lull at the front. It had a tar paper roof that sloped back like a lean-to, and narrow rectangular windows that faced the countryside. It was simply furnished, with a small dressing bureau, a cot, a table and two chairs; and to Calder, it was home.

Most of his free time was spent in his quarters with a bottle of fine wine and even a round of cheese sometimes, or a can of delicately seasoned fish. All of this, when circumstances and wit produced it, was kept in a thick wooden box that had been used to ship 105 howitzer fuses.

On nights that Calder considered special—for no other reason than the mood he was in—he would take a warm shower. Then back in his room, he would rub his body with a scented talc and lounge naked under a silken robe he had bought on the black market. Lying on his cot he would sip slowly from his glass of wine and eat small segments of cheese and fish. After long periods of reading he would lay the book down and sit dreamily by his window, watching the twilight on the countryside. From time to time he would caress his powdered body and pass his hand down into the slightness of his belly.

Before the alert the terror of combat was an idea that

had lived at the core of nebulous rumors, the tail end of
a distant horror that existed only in the urgency of voices
he heard over the phones and radios of the company de-
manding supplies. Sometimes he could feel it in the lists
of items he would receive and notate, and check and dou-
ble-check against the quadruplicate forms that filled his
filing cabinet and covered his desk like reams of news-
print. He remained indifferent to talk concerning the war,
but he felt a strong curiosity about enemy atrocities detailed in the films and slides shown at the weekly propa-
ganda sessions. And the proximity of the front lines, some
fifty miles to the north, had produced in him a languid
security mixed with a vague excitement.

After a time his notion of danger began to feed his joy
of being near it, and once, while reading in the rec hall,
he overheard a combat corporal and what the corporal
said made him listen closely.

". . . it took the whole company by surprise," the corporal was saying. "We're eating rations when it broke loose,
and a buddy of mine and some other guy and me dive into
this ditch. We lay in that hole clawing the dirt while
everyone ran looking for cover. It was the worst even the
seasoned guys had ever been under. It felt like the
ground was blowing up. Everything is flying—rocks,
equipment, vehicles, parts of bodies—everything. Even a
head comes rolling in on us with the helmet still strapped
on. I see a guy running for cover who gets cut apart at the
waist. Cut in two, from the belt up, right there in front of
me, his legs running for another ten yards like he was still
on them . . ."

Calder was impressed by the corporal's easy manner.
He stared admiringly at the muscular contours of his chest
and buttocks, the perfect tailoring of his O.D.'s, and the
long firm thighs that filled them out.

". . . but," the corporal went on, "when I woke up in

4 The Wine Cellar

the field hospital with my chest bandaged and find out I'm the only one out of the whole company who survived, I had this feeling."

"You were feeling guilty," someone said.

"Plenty of guys feel that," someone else said.

"Yeah," the first one said, "everybody gets that."

"No," the corporal said, "this was different because I had time to think about dying."

"About death, you mean?"

"No, about dying, but it had nothing to do with the war. With the situation, maybe, but not with the war itself."

Calder moved a little closer, but the corporal and his group fell silent.

After the story Calder went back to his room. He showered and rubbed himself with the scented talc. He sat in his robe by the window, sipping from his glass of wine. He stared at the countryside and it seemed to him now a landscape in a dream. The bare rigid poplars stood like a mesh of iron against the sky. The stream below them lay in a frozen glare, a strip of burnished steel in the winter light curving beyond his view, and where the snow had melted in the fields spreading white to the base of the hills, the earth showed through in black irregular patches, and he could see the outcroppings of broken rock and the clawlike branches of leafless bushes. Could he paint such a picture? Why not? he thought, and as he looked out over the countryside, the twilight began to shimmer like mirrors on the leaves of the big poplars. He could see it flicker in the stream that ran below the poplars; it highlighted the figures of his men who fished quietly from the banks. It shone on everything that moved: on the children of his workers who ran along the dirt paths and played in the cool shadows of the groves. It fell like a fine tinted dust upon the families of his workers who ate from their colored quilts lying in the grass. And farther down along the stream his fields opened up full to his view, stretching like a great carpet of growth to his wooded valleys and the range of his hills that rose in his imagination like distant monuments out of the shadows of dusk.

His hand passed over his powdered thigh. There is no reason to lie about how one felt under bombardment, he thought. Had he heard something true? Looking at his painting and sipping wine from the glass, he wondered how he might feel in the same situation. He leaned back slowly in his chair, his eyes closed, and let it come while he ate. When it came, he got up and showered again. He had one more glass of wine and ate a piece of cheese. Then, naked, he got into his cot, closed his eyes and slept.

In the days that followed, Calder became preoccupied with the details of what he had heard. At night he was unable to sleep. When the early hours finally weighed on his lids, he would drift off into a fitful drowse. During the day the work he tried to do only fed his confusion: his desk and filing cabinets became disheveled, he misplaced order forms, he left dozens of invoices unverified, and he fell behind in checking off his lists of priority items. Presently he began to spend his free time sitting near the door of the rec hall thumbing through magazines. When someone came in he would look up, hoping to see the corporal. In the mess hall he sat before cups of sour coffee, and watched for a glimpse of the youthful face in the shuffle of passing men. His meals, when he did eat, were perfunctory, and sometimes, weighted by his preoccupation, he sat forlornly until all who came had eaten and the chairs and tables stood empty in the silent hall. In the hope of a chance meeting, he took walks along the alleys that lay between the tin-walled storage sheds and the stacked rows of crated supplies. At night, cautiously, more than once, you could see him leaning off in the shadows, studying the faces of the guards standing inspection before taking up their posts.

One night, wracked by sleeplessness, Calder stepped out into a flood of glaring moonlight. He moved slowly down a path that lay between a row of occupied coffins waiting for shipment. Although covered, they had always been a vexation to him during the activity of the day. Now at night they appeared rueful in the sullen aura of the moonlight, rising on each side like a wall of rock under their draperies of frozen tarpaulins. A webbing of frozen ropes reached the full length of the stacks, and reeds of ice shone in the creases of the tarpaulins. As he looked moodily at the irregular patterns made by the gleaming ropes against the massive black bulk of the wall, it came with a realization that it wasn't real. At first, distant and sporadic in the deadening silence, the sound of artillery heightened gradually until the ground heaved under him, and strobes of light flashed above his head. It passed as suddenly as it had come.

Back in his quarters, Calder lay down on his cot. In the morning, he resolved, he would see the headquarter's sergeant. He would learn of the corporal's whereabouts. At this point, he thought sullenly, it was the only thing to do.

The sergeant looked up as if surprised when Calder introduced himself again. Sergeant Spine leaned back in his swivel chair and stretched out his arms, palms down and fingers stiff, to rest them on the edge of the desk in front of him. It was a movement perfected out of long practice.

"Calder? Sounds familiar," Sergeant Spine said, swinging back and forth in his chair. "But I can't seem to place you."

"Did you forget those extra blankets?" Calder said calmly.

"Yeah," the sergeant drawled. "You're the guy." He smiled sarcastically.

Calder steadied himself, and then he spoke. "I'd like to know where I can find a certain corporal."

"What's his name and serial number?" the sergeant said, leaning back in his chair.

"I don't know," Calder said.

"Just his rank?" the sergeant said. "That's all you know about him?"

"I know quite a bit about him," Calder said.

"What do you know about him?"

The question stopped Calder. He wanted to turn around and walk out.

"I can't trace a guy by his rank, Raymond," the sergeant said. "And I could have your ass in a sling just for standing there referring to classified information." The sergeant relaxed, took in a breath and said, "But tell me why you want this guy and I might be able to help."

Calder didn't answer. He thought about the question while the sergeant waited, turning from side to side in his chair, his arms folded across his chest, smiling. "What do you want with this guy?" the sergeant asked again.

"He's a stamp collector," Calder said. "I want information on a rare stamp. I'm sure he can give it to me." He relaxed now and added, "What's so classified about that, Sergeant?"

"What kind of stamps?"

"Plain ordinary stamps."

"You said it was rare. How can it be ordinary too?"

"Look, Sergeant, I could go over your head . . . "

"Hold it, Mr. Calder. No threats!"

"Sergeant," Calder said apologetically, "I simply want to find a man—boy, I mean—who can help me with his knowledge of stamps."

"Just don't go flying off, then. How valuable is the stamp?"

"That's the point," Calder said. "I've got to find out its origin and date, and other details . . . concerning its character, its . . ."

"What does he look like?" the sergeant interrupted, getting up from his chair. He walked to the filing cabinet on the far side of the room. While Calder described the corporal, the sergeant checked the files. It took less than five minutes to find Corporal Shane.

The sergeant held the folder open. "Nice-looking boy," he said, taking angular views of the picture.

"Yes," Calder said softly, "he is."

"Nice bright eyes. Complexion soft as a baby's ass." The sergeant closed the folder, moved to his desk and sat down.

"C'mere, Calder," the sergeant said.

Calder stood in place. The sergeant opened the folder again and studied the picture.

"What is it you really want with this Corporal Shane . . . this boy?"

"Stamps," Calder said.

"Corporal Shane!" Calder yelled again, this time with authority.

The corporal stopped in the path and turned around. "Me, sir?"

"Yes, you. Could I have a word with you?" Calder said, walking towards him.

They faced each other and Calder stared directly into his eyes. "About a month ago," he said, "I overheard you talking and would like to know more about it."

"About what?"

"About clawing the dirt," Calder said.

"Clawing what?"

"Dirt!" Calder stammered. "About the shelling and you clawing the dirt. Don't you remember?"

"I'm sorry. Perhaps it was someone else," the corporal said.

"It was you," Calder said.

The corporal looked down at the snow. "Yes, sir," he said solemnly.

"Would you like to talk about it," Calder said, "in my quarters?"

"If it doesn't take long," the corporal said.

A week had passed since they had had their talk, and Calder was sleeping soundly now. He put his desk and filing cabinets in order and he caught up on his invoices. At times he walked jauntily through the aisles of crates and boxes and through the stacks of metal ammo cans, joking casually with his men. Once he was seen on the loading platform, with his sleeves rolled up, standing in line, passing ammo cans hand to hand to the trucks.

He thought less and less of Corporal Shane. He sat now by his window dressed in his robe looking out to the countryside. His body was dusted with the scented talc and there was a distant look in his eyes. He ate his cheese as usual and drank his wine, and while he chewed, his hand found its object and moved with the rhythm of his jaw. When he got close he held himself back. Then, perfectly, with his eyes closed, he sipped delicately from his glass, swallowed at the precise moment, and sank into his chair exhausted.

The silence inside the truck disturbed him. The noise outside disturbed him. As if from a dream he heard the groan of laboring engines and the treads of half-tracks and tanks grinding off. Beside the roadway he saw groups of bloody stragglers bandaged and without weapons, some of them helmetless, standing like broken trees in the mist. All of this disturbed him, and he longed for his landscape and savored the memory of himself alone sipping wine.

But the hours passed and dusk slipped in with the fog. "Claw the dirt," he said to himself, his lips moving as if in prayer. With his eyes closed he sank back relaxed, filled with a new excitement. "Claw the dirt," he said again, this time aloud.

A few miles south of the city the roads were clogged with refugees. Calder watched as they were hustled into the nearby fields. Off from the rest stood a group of men, women and children clustered around a horse-drawn wagon. In a wicker chair at the rear of the wagon sat a bearded man whose heavy brown cape of fur, opened at the front, was draped from his shoulders. Calder stared absently at his white shirt with its high blue collar, and his black musty hat that was cocked to the side of his head. As the convoy pulled away, Calder watched the figure recede in the fog.

The convoy moved into the city a few hours before noon under a drizzling rain. There was chaos everywhere: hundreds of soldiers and aimless civilians moved through the streets. Jeeps, troop carriers, heavy armor and motorized artillery jammed the intersections. Calder ached with cold. He watched the rain streak through the snow of the passing weaponry. He listened to the tank treads ringing on the cobbles. From the bombed-out dwellings the shattered windows looked down at him like eyes in a blunted face. A deep confusion possessed him.

By mid-afternoon he had been issued a rifle and ammunition. Then, in a driving rain mixed with snow, he moved out with his company to take up positions on the defense perimeter.

It had been a painful march for him. He had crossed stretches of frozen fields, wound through torn trees and struggled in and out of small icy ravines. Now, with his pack off and wrapped in his poncho behind a boulder, his fingers worked hopelessly on the bolt of his weapon, trying to load it with a clip of thirty-calibre bullets. Once, he had almost pulled back enough on the bolt to insert the clip, but it snapped forward, catching his thumb as it slammed against the firing chamber. He stared at the copper heads of the bullets glinting with beads of mist. Cradling the rifle in his lap, he ran his finger over the cluster of copper heads pointing up from the base of the clip.

It wasn't long before he had one bullet free. Holding it, he thought its weight was unusually heavy for its size. Curiously, he took it with his thumb and forefinger and slowly moved his fingers up along the cartridge to the fierce tip of its head. Then he slid his fingers slowly down the brass shank to its base.

"It is a lead projectile!"

"Its shell is made of brass."

"It has a copper jacket streamlined to increase its velocity."

"Its penetrating force can take it through a half-inch plate of steel at six hundred yards."

"When fired it develops a muzzle velocity of twenty-five hundred feet per second."

"It can really move."

"It's accurate and deadly."

"If you shoot straight it will kill at a thousand yards. Any questions?"

Calder hadn't asked any questions that day, but he was on the rifle range with the rest of his company marking up scores that qualified him as a sharpshooter in less than a week. It was unusual and he knew it. "You just got the gift," his cadre had said. "Just got the gift."

Maybe it had been a gift, Calder thought modestly, or even a talent, or the fact that he had liked the sleek heft of the rifle balanced between his shoulder and arms. He had liked the tapering barrel set in its wooden stock. And he had liked the feel of his eye smiling through the peep sight where the bull's eye had wavered like a dot on a ballerina's stomach. He liked the snug fit of the tail stock in his shoulder, pressing in like a soft wedge before that one explosive instant when the mere pressure of his finger inspired the hammer home and fired the bullet off.

He looked at the bullet and remembered the proximity of flesh and hardware, sounding off cadence in the evergreen forests of Georgia. Holding the bullet to his eye now, the proximity of men came over him again. He tried to load his weapon and this time he succeeded. He was surprised by how much he remembered, and in one movement he had opened the bolt. He inserted the clip, pulled back on the bolt, thumbed it free and let it slam forward, setting his first round into the firing chamber. Then he put on the safety, zeroed his sights for an accuracy of one hundred yards, and like the rest of his platoon, he waited.

The first barrage ripped through the silence just before dark. Calder, with his head face-down in the snow, felt the life of his nerves. Over him passed rocks and clumps of frozen earth. He thought he would look up as the corporal had done, but instead, with both hands, he pulled his helmet closer against his head. "It will pass," he heard himself say. "It is a situation that will pass, and I will survive." After some time, as if a switch had been thrown, it was over.

He opened his eyes. He didn't know how long the shelling had lasted, but he saw that the light had faded and night had begun to sweep in with the fog that lifted from the draws and hollows a half-mile or so away. He smiled, felt a haunting excitement, and with his ears still numb from the sounds, watched the trees disappear and the slopes of the hills and the fields in front of him dissolve into the banks of fog. In a while the fog was on him. It covered him. He could see nothing now but the boulder and a patch of terrain on either side.

Beyond his line of sight he heard someone calling out orders. The voice was brusque and loud, and the men answering called off their names in turn along the line. When his turn came he answered. "Calder here!" he yelled, and he leaped to his feet. "Calder," he heard again, and he recognized the voice of Sergeant Spine.

Spine's face came through the fog, his mouth spread in a wide grin. He was visible now from his waist up, standing with his hands on his hips, his shoulders squared.

"Well, lookey here now," the sergeant said. "Mr. Warrant Officer Calder. Well, I'll be."

Calder drew the back of his hand across his mouth. "You'll be what?"

"Easy, honey. I just thought I'd never see you up here, is all." After a long pause the sergeant added, "How's it going, man?"

Calder answered curtly, his eyes set hard on the sergeant: "I can handle it," he said.

The sergeant ran his tongue over his lower lip. "Got through it all right?"

"Not a scratch."

The sergeant sniffed once and drew his finger under his nose. "Tell me," he said, moving up a little closer, "did you ever find your boyfriend?"

Calder said nothing.

The sergeant smiled. "C'mon, honey. No need for that up here," he said slowly, gently.

Suddenly small-arms fire opened up down the line. The sergeant spun around and looked off into the fog. "Here they come, sweet boy," he said, turning back to Calder, the grin never leaving his face. "Good luck, and la de da." With this he turned, shook his ass at Calder, and started off, his shoulders low and his head up, laughing as he moved.

The firing from both sides increased, rattling the air like nails on a sheet of metal. Calder didn't know how much time he had before the sergeant would disappear completely. He could still see his outline, a shadow stretched out on the ground taking cover. When the shadow lifted to move on again, Calder was already in position. He squeezed off five rounds in rapid succession, two across the outline and three down, the tip of his rifle barely moving an eighth of an inch in its pattern. The sergeant toppled like a sack gone empty. When he hit the ground, Calder laughed almost audibly, and pumped three more rounds into the sprawled-out form.

He woke cramped with cold. He ate a bit of canned sausage from his rations and then looked over the boulder. Stretched out in the fields were a dozen or more dead soldiers whose uniforms were powdered with snow. Farther down the field, where the ground sloped abruptly upwards into a grove of trees, he could make out other bodies lying in the leafage that had been mulched by gunfire. Toward the city the landscape was chopped and broken into rubble, and on a rise, less than a mile away, two treadless tanks still smouldered in the light. Beyond these and from the city itself smoke lifted like fists into the drifts of fog, but there was no sound. The wind too had diminished and the dawn light held the silence fast.

When he heard the whimper Calder looked around. He saw first the old man. Then from his fur cape the child's head appeared. She saw Calder, and brought her hand to her mouth. The rags about her head furled loose and her hair fell tangled into the folds of the cape. Calder figured her to be eleven or twelve.

The old man had not moved. His open mouth showed
the glimmer of scattered gold teeth. The lower part of his
beard had drawn to a point and was held stiff by webs of
frost. The fur of his cape was crystallized with nettles of
frost, and snow had filled the long folds. Calder knew he
was dead. Although the hat was missing, he recognized
the face.

Calder sat with his arm around her. He gave her pieces
of sausage which she ate until the can was empty. "Are
you afraid now?" he asked.

She had understood and shook her head. "No," she
said, "I am not afraid."

Calder stared quietly at the child. Getting up slowly, he
bent low and walked over to the old man. When he got
within reach, he applied pressure to the opened lids and
closed them. This done, he carefully shifted the body,
laying it down on the rubble. He pulled the cape over the
face and stood a while looking down at the legs. He
thought of pulling the cape back now and looking once
more at the face. He had seen no trace of blood or other
signs of a wound. His hand reached for the collar of the
cape. When his fingers took hold, the child screamed frantically. He turned from the old man's body and looked at
the girl. Stumbling to her, he reached out and cupped her
cheeks in his hands. "It's all right," he said. "You have
nothing to fear." He looked around, saw the wide stretch
of terrain, the ravines and the hollows, the frozen slopes
blanketed with snow and pocked with rubble. He put his
arm around the girl and brought her in close to himself.
In a while she was asleep.

He could feel the heat of her small head against his
shoulder. He could smell the scent of her hair. He concentrated on the closed lids and the dark brown lashes. Then
turning from her he looked off into the light drawing into
dusk. The silence spread like a cloud in the cold.

16 The Wine Cellar

When the barrage broke loose again, he raised his head slowly and looked into the glare of incendiary flares. He watched as other flares ignited and descended gracefully through canopies of light. Across the fields the distance was illumined by clots of glowing fires, and the muzzle explosions of heavy artillery ripped the darkness with bursts of flame. Calder watched the scene with awe. Suddenly he turned away and took his bayonet in his fists and looked at the girl.

It didn't take long. When it was over he drove the bayonet home once, twice, then again. He stood listening to her cries until they stopped. Then he listened, until he slept, to the exploding shells.

A Case in Point

The two women, dressed in identical denim jackets and faded blue jeans, parked their Land-Rover above the high-water mark, got out and ran down to Mason. He stood exhausted now by the rear wheels of his Kontiki camper that had spun into a mud hole where the lay of the beach sloped abruptly into a spread of sand flats. Some fifty feet out beyond the flats an oncoming tide drove before it a ridge of surf.

The two stared at Mason while he explained the reasons for his predicament. Neither seemed to hear what he had to say.

"Do you think all that talk was necessary," the tall one asked. Her voice had a deep hollow resonance as if it came through the end of a metal

pipe. She was heavyset with husky shoulders. Her
straight blond hair was cut short. Her eyes, severely
veined and watery, seemed on the edge of popping out.

Mason looked at her. "I've got to get out of here is all
I'm trying to say and I need help to do it."

"Giving you help is hardly a concern of ours," the short
one said. She spoke with the tempo of an hysteric. She
stood with her hands at her sides, rigid as wood, her
muscular legs swelling in her jeans. She too had close-
cropped, straight blond hair.

While the tall one watched Mason, the short one bent
down and studied the condition of the wheel. She gave a
quick arrogant tap to the half-exposed hub cap and stood
up.

"He literally ruined a good piece of beach," she said.

Now the tall one bent down to have a look. "I wonder,"
the tall one said, looking, "I wonder if he realizes the time
it took for nature to . . . " she rose slowly, wiping mud
from her elbows . . . "for nature to have made these al-
luvial deposits?"

Something of confusion and anger flushed into Mason's
face. He looked at the surf apprehensively. "I might know
what you mean," he said, turning back to them. "But
when the tide runs over my crime it'll smooth it out. Now
either give me a hand or get someone who can. There
ain't much time," he added.

"It's obvious he understands nothing," the short one
said.

"Like the rest," the tall one said.

"Who in hell are the rest?" Mason said.

"That isn't the case in point here," the tall one continued.

Mason felt a dryness spreading in his throat. "Damn it,"
he said, "it won't be in another twenty minutes, if that's
what you mean."

The tall one stuffed her hands into the back pockets of

her jeans and walked the length of the camper. She studied the chrome-plated weather stripping, the glaring aluminum walls, and the brand name, KONTIKI, a bold face row of slanted, four-inch golden decals above the door at the rear. KONTIKI. She stared up at it. Nodding her head disbelievingly, she turned and came back, forcing a quick smile that vanished the moment her lips went shut.

She looked into Mason's face. She pointed to the buggy tracks and the sign that enforced their use, "Up there, big boy . . . " she said, shaking her finger. "Up there is where you and your junk heap are supposed to be . . . in the tracks. You hear?"

"And if you had stayed up there," the short one said, accenting every syllable, "you wouldn't have gotten stuck down here."

There was a silence. Then with a sudden meanness the tall one said, "Do you know we have reason now to let you sit?"

"Until the tide takes you and your camper," the short one countered . . . She glanced at her friend. The friend glanced back at her.

"It makes little difference to me," the tall one said.

"Christ almighty," Mason said, "I don't believe it."

They smiled at each other and Mason knew they meant it. They would let him sit.

He thought a while. Finally, he said, "You're right, ladies. I should have stayed in the buggy tracks. Now that's elemental, and you have my deepest apology for that." He looked at the breakers boiling in. "But the flats appeared so untouched," he continued, "that I had to feel their existence under me." He paused and looked straight at them. "I ask you, can you blame a man for that?"

There was a tight silence this time. Then from the tall one, "Why didn't you walk down? Tell me that."

"Well, actually," Mason said, "I was going to. In fact, I

stopped first and got out." He pointed. "You see that huge gray log. That great, monumental log up there? Yes? Well, I sat on it and looked out over the ocean, and it seemed to me that eternity was symbolized in the expanse of blue right to the horizon. I said to myself, 'Mason, the color of eternity must be blue.' I tell you truthfully, ladies. It was a strange and beautiful feeling that came over me, and I had to get closer."

The two glanced at each other. Mason picked up his shovel, drove the blade into the sand and went on, "I can understand your concern for the purity of the beach," he said. "Yes, purity and peace. Two most significant elemental things." He looked out over the water now, his face an expression of solemn detachment, his head raised reverently. "Human roots," he said. "Roots of elemental purity crawling from the deep. But there are times, ladies, when nature takes no part in her drama. It's as if . . . as if she stepped aside sometimes to let things go on their own." He turned to them dead on and asked, "Do you believe that?"

A tense silence. Mason smiled softly. "Ladies," he said, "I can tell that you do believe it. Yes, indeed, you are as you say, a case in point."

It came on them like a wind, as his voice trailed off. There was not so much as an utterance from either when the blade of the shovel came down, first on the head of one, then the head of the other. Both fell like trees.

With the use of their Land-Rover, Mason hauled his camper free of the mud. He stood parked now in the buggy tracks that would lead him out to the main road.

Looking back, he mused on shards of driftwood, on wracks of kelp interspersed with sheaves of tangled weeds, and on the dead gray logs laid out randomly along the contours of the high beach. He listened to the surf pounding. He heard the freshening gusts of wind and sheets of sand rasping against the walls of the camper. It was all familiar to him, yet a dreary lassitude spread through him. Now his eyes followed the high-tide line. Some twenty yards into the water beyond it, he saw the roof of the Land-Rover awash in roils of foam. Immersed in the breakers falling near shore he saw the two bodies flopping hopelessly. With his eyes still on them he pulled in a deep breath of sea air. In a while his lassitude passed, and in a reassuring voice he said, "It's elemental. Yes, indeed, it's all pure and elemental." He smiled, settled back in his seat and drove off.

Fever

It was mid-September and Nat Seever's luck had been good, with seven stripers taken on bait and three on plug. They were adequate fish for this late in the season, averaging ten pounds, some slightly more. He knew after he had taken his second fish within minutes that he had found the feeding hole of a school holding close to the warmer water near shore. He would wait then for two hours, when the next tide would be full. If he got any strikes, or if he caught another, he would fish for two more hours after full tide, and then go to sleep. It would be a little over four hours of fishing, but it would be easy work, for he would have a full moon. The wind was lessening, and the water offshore to the hole would be calm. The ground swells too had decreased since the night before, and they would give little surf to work against when he made his casts.

Seever stood now above the beach in the dusklight looking seaward. He smiled, stroked his stubble of beard, and felt again the need to look at his fish. When he reached his camp in a grove of scrub oak and pine some fifty yards back from shore, he fed three small logs to his fire, sat down cross-legged before it, and looked at the stripers lying on a sheet of tarpaulin spread alongside his jeep. After four hours out of water they were still in almost perfect condition: there was no odor, no visible decomposition. They were still as perfect in form as if he had just pulled them from the sea. He watched the play of the firelight on their bodies. He studied the lateral lines of dark and light scales along the sides, receding and converging into a taper, and the taper fanning out acutely into the winglike shape of the tails. They lay stiffly, side by side, a row of pointed heads each with its one eye open to the firelight, the pupils clouded milky with fluid, but the stare insistent and frozen as if from a bead of glass. The belly of the nearest one exposed to the light of the flame was crystal white, and its composite pattern of interlocking scales glistened like slivers of bone. "Bone," Seever said, and he got up, not fully standing, his knees still bent, and moved within reaching distance of his fish. He drew his finger along the head of one and traced the outline of the eye, then continued tracing carefully along the head to the jaw and along the lower lip to the partly opened mouth. He pulled down on the lip and inserted his finger deep into the mouth. Farther back in the throat he could feel the tightness of the narrowing gullet and the cold residue of fluids. With his free hand he rubbed his stubble, smiled, and looked into the stare of the fish below his face, his finger now moving in and out of the mouth slowly. "Still moist," he said. "Even to the gullet. And no smell yet." He withdrew his finger, hearing the quick snap of suction close the gullet. He stood up, and walked out of the clearing to check once more on the weather.

The moon was now full to its rim, lifting out of the horizon like a stone disk above the water. A few stars were visible to the north, but a cloud bank had risen and swept up darkly to the clouds that still held motionless on the horizon inland. "It might be overcast," he said, "but it'll make no difference to me." Yes, they were in there, and overcast or not they were his for the taking. He would fish until he got them all, fish until he fished the ocean clean; if necessary, until he collapsed. He had been bit since his first fifty-pounder taken four months earlier from a chartered launch out of Cuttyhunk. Then a week later, he felt the need to fish again as he had felt the same need some years before to hunt black bear in Maine. At that time he had felt it like a purge in his bones after he had brought a female down with one shot through the base of her neck and watched the huge mass of fur, muscle and head rise like a statue under the limb of an oak tree; watched the labor of her movement and the thick head rearing still upward with her mouth open in the circle of his scope; yes, watched the movement as if in a trance and felt his pleasure begin in an instant that held him full with excitement and laughter, a sound of laughter that was severe against the sound of splitting wood when she took the limb in her teeth, groaning still upward in her last movement, before he shot again, then again and again until his rifle was empty and he had brought her down, brought her five hundred pounds crashing down with the limb still in her teeth. Then—a week after Cuttyhunk and his first striper—he knew he had been bit; and he fished alone now as he had hunted alone whenever he got the chance.

Seever was no amateur after Cuttyhunk. He took a fifty-pounder out of the Cape Cod canal on a monofilament line of forty-five-pound test. He carried a picture of the bass balanced in his right hand held above his head; and his raw muscular arms, his small waist and bulging buttocks, his long thick legs, even his hands with their thick fingers, all indicated a strength that could have pressed three hundred pounds, a strength that could have broken a man's back with ease, or if concentrated in his fist held like the head of a mallet at his side, could have shattered a jaw.

The stripers Seever caught on the next tide in the flood of moonlight that he had wished for averaged over twenty pounds. He had worked farther out over the hole and had pulled in four. Later in camp before going to sleep he loaded his spool with a line of thirty-five-pound test. He resolved that he would go to an even lower weight if the fish got bigger. He would go to the lowest limit of what line he had, which was twenty-pound test, and he planned to use it on his nine-foot rod. The decision to use the lighter tackle was not impulsive; it was made after he figured his chances against the increasing easterly wind and the heavier surf that had developed on the falling tide just before he quit. It had been made for the same reason as his decision earlier in the year before Cuttyhunk: When his excitement for hunting had ceased, he knew he lacked the purpose and need for making repeated easy kills. The lighter tackle now, he reasoned, would prove his new ability against the odds of the heavier fish.

The following night, before the tide was full, he caught his biggest fish on the thirty-five-pound test line. It read exactly forty pounds on his scale. He fought it for near to an hour and a half, standing waist-high in the surf. At times the sea broke against his chest, and the sand beneath his feet was carried away in the backwash, leaving him balanced on the heels of his boots as if he stood on a floating rail. But Seever had worked his fish carefully, playing its weight delicately through the feel of his rod, feeling the stretch of line to its mouth and to the barb of the hook holding in the mouth. As he worked up and down the beach in the driving surf, he thought too of the hook holding deep through the fish's upper lip and protruding hard between the openings of its nose; thought he could see the eyes of the fish move like turrets of light in the murk of the water, staring like beads of glass on the curve of steel it had swallowed. Yes, Seever had worked his fish carefully, lost his footing once and went under. But he held on, came up and regained his balance without having let go of the rod. He felt then the initial force of the fish's mass and anger, and he felt his own anger while he reeled in, bucked the sea with his big chest and shoulders, sending just enough delicate pain to the hook when the striper had turned, feigned back toward shore and headed out again tiredly for the last time against the drag of his reel. And as the fish tired, so Seever's anger diminished and his laughter spewed from his soaking frame like the roar of a fire, high and severe above the roar of the surf as if he had conquered a nightmare of devils. The next night he went to his thirty-pound test.

The fish Seever had caught after five nights of fishing amounted to sixty school bass, twelve twenty- to thirty-pounders and the forty-pounder. He had caught three large skate about three feet across, which he had pulled in only to retrieve the hook. He considered the skates useless, and the lack of excitement he experienced when he caught them, the time wasted in removing the hook which was taken deep into the gullets, was not worth the loss of bait. Neither did he have any luck with the lighter tackle in taking a striper bigger than his forty-pounder. All of this, the skates and his increasing dissatisfaction with small fish, had triggered his anger and at times cramped his ability to make his casts accurately over the line of surf to the hole.

The fish he had caught—except for the forty-pounder, which he had carried up above the high-water mark and had covered with wet seaweed—were left on the beach. The six that he lived with in camp were thrown out into the clearing beyond the grove. Those he had left out in the open, torn at during the day by gulls and terns, were mutilated out of shape and shredded through to their entrails.

In his activity of fishing, keeping camp, and digging for bait while he waited for the tides, Seever was unconcerned with the carcasses lying along the beach, and by the end of the week the odor of rotting fish hung palpably in the air. But he worked the hole methodically at each tide. If he landed a striper over his forty-pounder he would go to the limit of his tackle, fish until he landed a bigger one, and then leave.

So Seever fished for two nights before he landed a striper that weighed forty-eight pounds. He had little difficulty and took it within an hour in a low rolling surf. After this he went to his light tackle. He caught school bass and a few more skates and several large cod and flounder which he threw up with the others. While he fished the daytime tides, the beach behind him was alive with yelping gulls, terns, and sheldrakes that had landed to feed on their way south. Against this background of noise, and in the stench which now carried even to his campsite, Seever fished, and he waited.

It was twelve-thirty in the morning. The half-moon shone through an expanse of open sky and lit a path across the water. In front of him, as if powdered with a fine covering of snow, the beach was visible in the light. Inland he could see the range of dunes like mounds of chalk, and the marshes spreading black to the inlet where he had dug more bait that afternoon. He stood fixed now above the beach, with his pole at his side and his gaff-hook hanging from his waist. His rubber waders, his boots, and his parka glinted in the moonlight. The vertical mass of his frame, with its thick head and face raised above his chest, was like a silhouette of wood, immobile and singular on the lay of the sloping beach and against the shifting expanse of water in front of him. With his pole held off the sand, and the stench of the rotting fish laced heavily in the force of the breeze that swept about him, Seever moved down the grade of beach across some five feet of remaining flats and entered the water smiling. It was three hours before full tide. With a minimum of ground swells the surf was irregular, running no more than a foot high over the flats and tonguing smoothly up to the edge of sand that marked the beach behind him. Once in the water he made his first cast toward the hole, and after an hour's fishing, he landed three. From their size he figured they weighed at least twenty pounds. His anger increased and he considered them as useless as skate.

There was no warning. When the fish struck it struck totally, bending the rod down to its butt end. Seever leaned forward to release the tension. "The drag must have jammed," he yelled. "If the bastard's gone, I'll . . ." The drag had jammed, but he had it working in seconds. The line drew taut down through the eyes of the rod, with four feet or more of it spinning off from the spool of the reel, and he knew he still had him. He let the line pay out over his finger, and felt the heft of the butt end in his hands. From this he calculated the fish to weigh at least sixty pounds, maybe a little more. He then cranked the reel until the line took up against the drag. When he secured his footing, he began the play.

Seever gave the fish no advantage, gave it no more
tension of line than enough to give himself the feel of its
position in the dark somewhere out beyond him. Once he
thought of moving up on shore, playing the fish from
there and then gaffing it while still in the backwash; but
he resolved finally to work it first over the line of the
breakers some fifty yards out and then move up to the
beach when it started its final run seaward from the shallow water near shore.

After two hours had passed, the fish was still in the
water. Seever began to feel the stiffness in his arms, the
cramping muscles of his legs, and the increasing inflexibil-
ity of his wrists each time he eased back on the rod. But
he continued to work carefully, rhythmically, moving with
the fish down-surf when it fought for more line. His head
was matted with soaked hair, his shoulders and chest laboring beneath his parka slicked smooth with water, and
all of him, the head rearing high above his chest, the
laboring shoulders, and the arms braced out straight from
the shoulders to the gripped hands around the butt end of
the rod, all of him down to his waist and to his buttocks
that showed hard against the strain of his waders in the
backwash—all of him contiguous with the movement of
water about him. And now as he reeled in on each down-
stroke of the rod he cursed aloud to the increasing wind
and to the spray, lifting like pellets of sleet out of the
driving surf. But he knew it would not be long. The fish
was tiring.

When a half hour more had passed he could see the
striper lying half up on its side in the crests and wallowing
closer to shore on each successive wave. Seever let it
come then, reeling in slack until he saw it leap out of the
water, arching from the end of the leader down, a curve
of muscle and scales flashing once in the moonlight, then
turning seaward in its leap. When it fell to the water
Seever was laughing, and again his laugh was severe and

high above the roar of the surf. "Bastard, I've got you," he yelled, and he moved up backwards out of the surf onto the shoreline. When the striper began its last run in the shallow water, he was ready. He started to give it line, all the line its run would take, no tension, no heft or pull, no weight, all slack and freedom on its run seaward before he would take it back with one final pull on the rod.

When the drag jammed again, Seever had only seconds to make his choice. Within the period of those seconds, and with the anger swelling in his chest, he followed up on his first choice: he let go of the rod, and in one movement was in the water with his arm around the striper's girth and his free fist like a sledge coming down upon its head. He wrestled it; it shook under him, bouncing like a coil spring snapped free from its mounts, slapping the sand with its tail, flanks, belly and head, its eyes like chips of crystal in the moonlight flashing on the angle of its stare. And as Seever fought his fish in the shallows of the surf he felt its weight of sixty-five pounds or more in the wash of sand, gravel and stone when the sea pulled back to leave it higher yet than the first shock of land against its flesh.

The first blow of his gaff-hook cracked deep into the striper's head. The second blow was halfway down when the wave came up. It rose hissing, broke, and then fell with a suddenness that held Seever immobile and useless under its weight. When it receded the fish was gone. The rod, too, with its tangled line was gone, and he stood in the wake of the wave's backwash exhausted. He felt the pain now in his right arm just below the elbow. When he saw the sleeve of his parka ripped open, he knew he had been cut. He knew with anger too it had been the horny, spikelike cartilage in the striper's dorsal fin that had cut him. In the moonlight he could see the slash and his blood pulsing out of it. He stared at it absently. "I should have killed him," he said. He gripped his arm and applied pressure, and without picking up his gaff-hook, he headed back to camp.

The next morning after packing his gear into the jeep, Seever returned to the shoreline and picked up his gaff-hook. Then he walked to the ridge of the beach where it sloped upward a few feet into a mound of compass grass, holly and tangled briar. In one movement he swung up the bank and stood in the grass, his eyes narrowing and his jaw set hard above the lapel of his open jacket. The cut in his arm throbbed under its dressing, but it was not unbearable. He looked a long time over the spread of sand below him. He could see the forty-pounder uncovered now and rotting, and the torn carcasses of the other stripers putrefying. His eyes held a while on the cartilage that had turned yellow in the open sides of their heads. Seever smiled. The odor of dead flesh hung like a shroud above the beach. Along the high-water mark he could see mounds of seaweed and the bones of the flounder and cod, and kelp and the weed mixed with sand, more mutilated fish and the black casings of skate eggs. Overhead a few remaining gulls hawked intermittently, soared and dipped in the sunlight. He looked up at the gulls. After a while, as if he had forgotten something, he faced the beach once more and smiled again. "I slipped," he said. "That's all." Then he turned away and with his gaff-hook and chain swinging from his fist, he walked through the briar, through the grass, back to the grove of scrub oak and pine, to his jeep.

Beginner's Luck

They had shot by in schools, hit fast and vanished, leaving the water lulled. By mid-afternoon they started hitting again, and Thorson, although a little tired, went after them with a fervor. He didn't see the father and son come up.

The two looked at him while he kneeled on the granite stones of the jetty baiting his hook. Each was the replica of the other, thin-boned and lanky with hard blue eyes and stiff red hair.

"We've been watching you," the father said. He wore a black coat sweater with leather patches on the elbows. His white shirt underneath, soiled gray and opened at the collar, exposed the blanched hairless skin of his chest.

"You've been having a lot of luck," the boy said.

He was about seventeen. A lock of hair half covered one eye. A baseball cap with a softened peak lapped down on his forehead. His eyes, when Thorson looked at him again, seemed unreal in the pallid face. It was as if two lusterless beads had been stuck in a plate of porcelain. His cheap plastic-housed reel, like his father's, glinted in the sunlight.

The father motioned to the boy with his head. The boy, without taking his eyes off Thorson, reached into his bait can and lifted out a handful of Thorson's oil smelts.

"Put them there," the father said, pointing to a chink in the granite. He turned to Thorson. "They don't seem to like no jigs so we thought we'd borrow some bait."

Thorson finished baiting his hook. He stood up.

"That is, if you don't mind," the father added.

Thorson cast out. "I don't mind," he said. In a while he worked another fish, its belly tilted half up on its turn, swimming at a right angle to the line slicing the water, like the fuselage of a small jet. The father watched. A slow thin smile spread across his drawn face.

"Some have it, some don't," he said in a clipped nasal voice. "But we gonna show we have it too."

On his first cast the line fell short, plunging like a rock into the water. On his next cast the bait let go, landing some ten feet beyond the line's drop. In a swirl of broken water it was taken on the surface and the fish, visible for an instant, turned in a flash of sunlight and shot away. Eyeing Thorson, the father cursed through a row of broken teeth, and cast again.

The three fished from a section of the jetty where the granite flattened out for some ten feet in length. More than once their lines tangled. The father and the son used inordinately heavy sinkers and hooked bottom on all but a few of their casts. Once, in his attempt to pull free under his father's directions, the boy varied the angle of the line by walking back and forth along the ten feet of granite, pulling nervously on his rod and tripping over Thorson's bait can. Finally, he pulled free, and disregarding Thorson's suggestion to use a lighter sinker—or none at all since the fish were hitting near the surface—he drew the rod back over his head in a sweeping arc and cast again; but the line backlashed on the spool of his reel and snapped in towards the jetty, the hook end passing less than an inch under Thorson's eye.

"God Jesus Almighty," Thorson said.

"He created all the creeping things," the father said.

"He created all the fish and fowl too," the boy said.

"So you don't own the ocean," the father said.

"And he don't own the fish in the ocean either," the boy said.

"So the worthy will inherit shit," Thorson said. Cramped by anger in making his casts effective he considered calling it a day, but as he reeled in, the fish struck with a jolt. He adjusted his drag and began the play.

Carl Thorson hadn't fished in five years. It wasn't because he lacked the time. His interest had simply faded. Feeling the presence of the father and the boy like a weight pressing on him, he could remember those long hours in the past, fighting surf on hopelessly deserted beaches. He could remember the small miseries that could taunt one while casting into empty water, waiting for that one consummate strike that would make it all worth it. He could remember that the fish had been sizeable at times, like the raging ten-pound blue he had fought for near to an hour with critically light tackle in a biting wind off the Jersey coast one late September. Taking a glance at the father and the boy, he remembered now, with embarrassed modesty, the fifty-five-pound prize striper he had landed at Montauk Point.

Watching, the father and the son stood like two spectral

shapes on the huge granite slabs of the jetty. When they saw the fish break water, their mouths dropped open. A solid pound or two, the big mackerel hung in space on a node of light, fell to the water, sounded and headed out.

"He's got the luck for the big ones too," the father said. He smiled through a fierce silence and waited. The son beside him stood no less fierce in the replica of his mold.

At first, Thorson understood the feeling that came over him only in its vaguest physical sense, like the pull of gravity on a stone. Working the fish, he tightened his grip on the butt of the rod as if it were the handle of an axe. If I land it, he thought, they'll hate me for it. Applying more drag, he snapped the tip of the rod as he would have snapped the end of a whip. But the line held, and the feeling seemed as ponderous in him as the rocks he stood on. "Either way, then," he muttered through his teeth. "Either way and the bastards lose." Thorson held the rod with one hand and, with the other, drew the knife out of the leather sheath slung at his side. He reached out to cut the line, but the boy, who had moved in close to stop him, lunged for his hand.

For an instant that seemed incomprehensible, there was the glare of metal in the sunlight as Thorson pulled the knife back and felt the tendons in the boy's wrist melt against the blade. While the boy sunk to the granite, the knife, as if by its own force, rose in his hand again and leveled at a point just above the father's heart.

The small group had collected around the prostrate boy. Thorson stood off to the rear and watched the dressing of the wound in silence. The two policemen had been called by a local who had seen the accident. After their questioning, the boy was lifted onto the stretcher. He looked directly at Thorson, and as if to make his pain visible to them all, his eyes narrowed accusingly in his bitten face. The father, too, had looked at Thorson with the same intolerable stare. But Thorson, unable to meet their eyes dead on, gazed absently at the knife lying on the granite.

As the small procession made its way down the long stretch of stone to the waiting ambulance, he picked up his knife and stood alone on the huge granite slab of the jetty and watched. He watched the stretcher sway between the glaring white figures of the ambulance attendants. He watched them work into position at the rear of the ambulance, watched the stretcher slide in and saw the massive red and white door slam closed behind it. He watched the father too, a gaunt figure in his black sweater and long black pants, turn suddenly towards the jetty on the pivot of his thin waist, hesitate before the opened door of the police cruiser, turn suddenly again, bend his gangling frame and stoop inside. With a joy that seemed to nibble in his chest now, he watched the ambulance and the police cruiser disappear into a grove of trees that hid the road. All of this he had watched with an inkling of remorse fading through him like a dying shiver. The fact that no charges were brought against him meant nothing to him. Still he felt a little confused, but eating the fish he was sure would cure that. He was sure, too, it would cure any memory of his rage, which even now had diminished to a trembling in his hands. He picked up his gear, slung the sack of mackerel over his shoulder and headed for shore. He did not look back.

Kopect's Story

They had talked most of the night. Early the next morning the patrol officer who had arrested Tibbs for vagrancy looked through the bars of the cell and explained to him and Kopect that they would be taken to the courtroom at eleven for trial.

The officer left and Tibbs stretched out on the wooden bench suspended from the wall. He rested his head on his shoes that served as a pillow, and stared pensively up at the ceiling. He wondered what would happen in the courtroom and the penalty he would have to face. After a while he leaned up and looked over to Kopect, who was making himself comfortable on the hopper he used as a chair.

"What do you think they'll do to me, Kopect?" he asked.

"Probably pay a fine is all. Or they might change the charge to idle and disorderly behavior. Nothing to worry about," Kopect said. He was in his late fifties. He had gray curly hair and a short gray beard. His eyes were unusually large, flashing blue and clear in the diffused light coming into the cell. His face was tanned deeply and he had high cheekbones and full red lips which protruded slightly beyond the hair of his beard.

"I wonder if they reached my father for bail?"

"Would make no difference now anyway," Kopect said.

"What do you think the fine will be?"

"Can't say. Depends on the judge."

Tibbs sat up now and swung his feet onto the floor. "Did you have a hard time in prison when you were there?" he asked quietly.

"Damn right. As I told you last night, I did two-and-a-half years for going AWOL before I shipped overseas. You see," he went on, "I was in the army four years before the Second World War started and they released a lot of us to fight. Was glad to get out of that hole too," Kopect said wearily. "Strange place to spend time in. Strange guys there."

"What do you mean?" Tibbs asked curiously.

"Well, I'm not sure I should tell you."

"Why not?" Tibbs said, laughing.

"What happened to me in prison I never told anyone. Why should I tell you?" Kopect looked away and rubbed the side of his face.

"It'll make the time go by."

"Nervous?"

"No."

Kopect thought awhile. He fingered his beard and stared down at the floor. "Maybe I should tell you," he said, looking up at Tibbs again. "Might make me feel better about it."

"I'll never repeat it if that's what you're worried about, Kopect, believe me."

"I've been coming to this town a long time, kid, and a lot of people know me. Hate to see it get around." Kopect rubbed his face again. "I make my living here in the summer, you know." He rubbed his eyes now and then looked across at Tibbs. "It has to do with a homosexual," he said.

"So what, Kopect? I mean . . . "

"Well, I'm not queer," Kopect broke in.

"I didn't think you were."

"Well, I want to get it straight that I'm not and never was."

"It would make no difference anyway; I wouldn't tell if you were."

"I just want you to know I'm not."

"What happened in prison then?"

"Well, like I say, I did time in a compound for going AWOL. But after they got me trying to escape they sent me to a federal prison and there were guys there from buggers to arsonists. Couple of guys for attempted murder and deserters from the First World War they never executed. Everybody, I tell you. But I fit right in, and I say to myself, Henry, you're going to make out all right if you mind your business. So the first couple of months go by easy. Then I start to get bored. I was only a kid then, don't forget. As tall as I am now but skinny, and the other guys, some of them I mean, would pat me on the ass now and then and to tell you the truth, I began to like it. There was a lot of buggery going on. I never saw it happen though, but I could feel it like you know someone is watching you but you don't see them. I knew it by the way the older guys looked at me and patted my ass when I walked by or even touched my face with their hands and squeezed my cheek sometimes. They were dreamy kind of guys, I remember. Most of them were tall and very muscular and you could tell they knew the ropes. They seemed to have found a home there. They seemed dreamy and happy and all the time there was a smile on their mouths. Well, I got horny after the first three or four months and started jerking off a lot—almost every night, after I knew the other guys were asleep. Each of us had our own cell and you could talk back and forth. You could even hear each other taking a dump in the little toilets they had in the cells. Anyway, I started jerking off more and more. Then one night when I was laying back kind of taking my time with it, I hear this guy in the next cell. I could tell by the way he was breathing and sighing and by the little moans he was making that he was maybe jerking off too and I wondered if he could hear me. We went on like this for about a half hour. I held myself back about four times and started to get so close to coming that it began to hurt. What I could hear wasn't loud. And it wasn't fast either. I guess I really didn't know he was jerking off because I could just about make out these sounds. I guess I was only suspicious or—I don't know how to say it—hopeful maybe that he was. So after I hear him like that, when I first hear him working it up like that between my own strokes, I stop. Then I lay back and listen and I hear him stop the same time I do. Well, after I hear him stop I was sure then he was jerking off, and with me, and I began to wonder about something. It was a strange feeling. And when I squeezed my own thing and leaned up to look at it I swear I could feel its size in my mouth. I gave it a few more hard strokes, fast like, as though I was going to bring it off, and the springs squeaked under my ass about four times. Well, I stopped and listened again and I'll be a son of a bitch if his bed didn't squeak four times too and then stop right after me. Then something went through me. It was an excitement I never felt before. I looked at my thing again and when I did this time it seemed it didn't belong to me, and believe me I felt the same feeling in my mouth."

Kopect was breathing heavily now and his face reddened. "I shouldn't tell you about this, I guess," he said quietly.

"It's OK," Tibbs said. "Besides, I won't ever see you again after we get out, so what difference does it make?" Tibbs leaned forward on the slab. "Go on if you really want to talk about it."

Kopect looked at him and smiled. "You're a funny kid," he said.

"What do you mean?"

"I don't know. It's just that I've never talked about this to anyone and here I'm spilling it out on you."

"It's the closeness," Tibbs said, smiling.

"Yeah, I guess so—or something—because I don't feel ashamed to talk to you about it. I think you understand." Kopect wiped his nose. "Well, after I hear this guy's bed squeak and I have this feeling in my mouth, it was quiet for a while and I began to feel a kind of horny I never felt before. As I said, I suspected the inmates were doing their buggery. I guess it was accepted in good taste because no one ever talked about it. Even this guy in the next cell—I knew he heard me and we both knew what was happening during the night but never said it outright to each other the next day. Not even after it got to be something with us. As a matter of fact this guy never talked to me much. He was a quiet type. Never talked much to anyone. He was dreamy too like I say, but he never smiled like the others. He had blond hair. It was really like a rusty color with blond streaks in it, always combed straight back. And it was thick. He used to stare a lot and move slow and do things like he was in a dream. When he talked to you, though—as I say he hardly ever did—he seemed to know exactly what you were going to say. He had blue eyes. And I mean a real blue—as if they were fake. Blue like the sky. I mean it. And narrow. Close together. He had bushy eyebrows and they were really blond like the streaks in his hair. Strange in a way. Bushy as hell. He was tall, too, lanky, about six feet I guess, maybe a little more, and his head was bony as if you could see the shape of his skull under his face. But his skin was clear and smooth just like a woman's, and it was always pale and the guy never shaved. But the thing that really struck me was he had no buttocks. At least they didn't show through his pants. The back of him was flat. But there was always a bulge at his crotch. When he walked his hips never moved. His legs seemed to swing from his hips and his toes would step out one right in front of the other like he was walking on a tight rope. He'd look right at me when we were being lined up for breakfast in the morning outside the cells. He'd stare for a long time with his blue eyes and they seemed always clear. Kind of a sparkle in them. Fresh like. Then he'd start moving his crotch in and out at me with its big bulge, back and forth, slow, like he was screwing something. He'd do this and keep his eyes closed and open his mouth too, just a little so I could see the tip of his tongue licking inside like. I'd look right back at him, though, while his eyes were closed and he knew I was watching him too because he'd sigh a couple of times and open and close his mouth. Then he'd open his eyes again, and when he did, they'd be staring right at me. I swear he could see through his lids." Kopect played with his beard. A moment passed, then he looked dreamily at Tibbs. "You know," he continued, "one morning while he was doing these things I began to feel embarrassed or ashamed, I guess, because I started to think this guy was really strange or was crazy."

"Why?"

"Well, we had a busy time the night before and I en-
joyed it good with him . . . must have come about three
times. But I tell you, I mean the things you can think
about in the dark, when you're alone at night in bed in a
cell jerking off listening to another guy jerking off. It's
strange. Besides, it seemed I shouldn't have let myself go
the night before, and I couldn't remember those things in
the morning that went on in my head while we made it
with each other. So when his eyes were closed on this
particular morning and he did these things with his mouth
and his tongue, sighing too and sucking like, I laughed
under my breath. I'm positive he couldn't have heard me,
but I was grinning hard thinking what a crazy bastard he
was after all. Well, when he opened his eyes again the
sparkle was gone. Believe me, they looked dry as a bone
and there was a stare from them that was hateful. I have
never seen anything like it before. And then his lips tightened and he smiled and it was the strangest smile I had
ever seen." Kopect breathed heavily now. He wiped his
mouth and shook his head. "Remember, I told you he
looked like a woman," he went on quickly. "Well, with his
eyes staring at me this way and with this smile on his lips,
smirking like, his features changed. It was the weirdest
face I ever saw, kid. Like an old man's. Believe me, it was
cruel and I was scared shit. But I was scared mostly because I was sure he knew what I had been thinking. I was
sure he saw me grinning through his eyelids. He stood
there staring at me for about ten seconds, and it was a
long time, believe me. Then just as fast, his face turned
back into like a woman's. Like it always was, and I swear
to god that during that time he was looking at me I felt I
was being murdered and I had seen the devil."

Kopect sat silently on the hopper shaking his head.
Tibbs remained quiet looking at him. After a while Kopect
unloosened his laces and took off his shoes. "You know,"

he said, his voice calmer now, "it was never the same after that, what me and this guy had together."

"What do you mean?" Tibbs asked. He leaned up on the bench with his hand against the side of his head for support.

"It changed between us," Kopect said.

"Did you do it again with each other?"

"Yes. And I got to hate him," Kopect said morosely. He played with his shoe.

"Why'd you hate him?"

"I don't know. I never hated anyone like that. What I should say maybe is I began to enjoy it in a different way. That's when it got worse." Kopect dropped his shoe. "It started the night after he looked at me that way, when I was sure he saw me through his eyelids and knew what I was thinking. I was laying back playing with myself and listening, I began to think too that maybe this guy wasn't crazy after all. I don't know why I thought this, but I felt I shouldn't have laughed at him. Not even under my breath. I mean, to each his own. You know?"

"I think so."

"After all, it's tough in prison without women around."

"Yeah," Tibbs said, "but what about that night?"

"Well," Kopect went on, "I was playing with it and listening in the dark waiting to hear from him. I even gave off a few loud sighs to make sure he could hear me. I wanted to get it going with him. More so now than ever before, but he wouldn't answer me. There was nothing coming back."

"Maybe he wasn't in his cell."

"I knew he was there. I saw him go in the same time as the whole block went in. All the cells close shut together, but if they wanted to, they could open any one alone. I would have heard them if for some reason they wanted to take him out. They did this to guys sometimes." Kopect looked down at his shoes. "No," he said, shaking his head, "he was in there all right, but the son of a bitch wouldn't answer me. And I wanted it so bad that night because I felt for the first time close to something I was never close to before, when I thought of how his face had changed in front of me that morning."

Kopect picked up one of his shoes. He looked at it. His face was grave, and when he spoke again he seemed to be talking to himself. "He knew I wanted it," he said softly. "The bastard was killing me for what I had done. That's why he wouldn't answer me. He saw me grinning at him and he knew I was thinking he was crazy. I tried all night to get it going again. I jerked off three or four times, and waited in between for him to make it with me. I looked at him the next morning too and he did the same thing with his face, the son of a bitch, and his big bulge moving in and out at me from behind his pants. I couldn't help it, believe me, I got so horny I came hard right there standing outside the cell while he sucked his pretty mouth and made those little sighs so I could just about hear them. I wanted to kill the bastard. I can't relax when I think of it." Kopect rubbed his face. Tibbs watched the hand move against the stubble on his cheeks and then across his chin and mouth. There was a web of mucus under Kopect's nose. Tibbs watched him sniffle and wipe the mucus off with the back of his sleeve. "Bothers me sometimes like a bad dream. It can stay with you and you don't know why —after you're awake—and there's nothing you can do to get rid of it." "It's shitty, I tell you."

"You feel like you dreamt it? What that guy did to you, I mean?"

"Shit no. That was no dream. It was real, believe me. He kept it up for a month every goddamn night, not doing it with me and he knew I wanted it bad. Thought I'd crack up, I tell you."

"Must have been frustrating," Tibbs said.

"In a way it was. In a way it wasn't," Kopect said. "I tried to get it going again, as I say, but I began hating him more for not making it with me. I knew he heard me and I began to get the hornies even better by jerking off and hating him at the same time for not answering me." Kopect played with his shoe, turning it over in his hand slowly. "But I liked it," he said, not looking at Tibbs. "I began to imagine things and I liked it."

"What'd you think about?"

"That's the part I don't want to think about. It's the part like when you're awake after a dream and can't forget it, but you don't know what the dream was."

"Why do you want to forget it?" Tibbs asked.

Kopect shifted himself on the hopper. "It's that I'd like to forget what I did to that guy later—after I began to imagine things."

"What'd you imagine, Kopect?" Tibbs was uneasy but he wanted to hear.

"Well, this guy's name was Karrens. I don't know why I didn't tell you his name before but I didn't think of it." Kopect picked up his shoe again and crossed his knees. "When I jerked off those nights hating him," he continued, "I had that feeling in my mouth again and I began to imagine things. Like I said, I felt close to something that's hard to explain. I liked hating him, and when I came off hating him it was the best I ever had. It was better, I tell you, than anything I had ever had with any woman. I could feel it everywhere. My whole body felt it, and when it was over, when I couldn't do it anymore, I fell off to sleep. It was a peace, I tell you."

"So why'd you want to forget that?"

"That ain't what I can't forget. It's what I did to Karrens later and I don't know why."

"What'd you do?" Tibbs asked.

Kopect turned his head away. "I beat him. And bad," he said quietly. "They put me in solitary for two months for it. Didn't think I could make it."

"Did he squeal on you?"

"No. They caught me in the shower room with him. You see, Karrens worked in the library and had a lot of freedom. He was a trusty and could take a shower whenever he wanted to. The rest of us used to take showers every other day at a certain time. Well, I got him one morning after he pulled that stuff on me outside the cell."

"But you said you got the hornies from it."

"I did, but I still didn't like it."

"Should've just told him to leave you alone," Tibbs said.

Kopect looked at Tibbs blankly now. "He was in the clinic for two months healing after I got through with him," he said. "I saw him in that shower room, and when I did, I sneaked back after him. We had just finished showering—the guys that worked in the machine shop, I mean—and while we were dressing, Karrens comes in and I watch him go into the room where everyone undressed. There were no doors separating the rooms, so I left the main one where all us guys were and I get him right under the shower." Kopect picked up his shoe again. "Actually though, all I remember is wanting to talk to him. I still wanted to see if I could get it going again. I was willing to give it a try." He began turning the shoe over in his hands. "But when I saw him naked," he said, "I guess I lost my head."

"What'd you do?"

Kopect stared down at the floor, his head lowered almost to his chest. "What I told you about his thing was a lie," he said. His voice was shaky. "I mean," he went on, "it wasn't as big as I thought it was. He must have stuffed something down into the front of his pants to make that bulge in front those mornings. When I looked into that shower, I saw him naked as a baby. I tell you all he had there between his legs was a little knob of flesh no bigger than your thumbnail. Smaller even. And he had no balls or hair either. Just scar tissue all the way up to his stomach—and flat too—like he had been burned. When I looked at him he tried to hide himself, and all I remember from then on is getting my hands around his throat and feeling the hot water soaking through to my skin. I guess I came close to killing him before they got me."

Kopect's eyes were closed. Tibbs thought he was going to cry. The two sat without speaking. Then Tibbs reached out and put his hand on Kopect's shoulder. "Kopect, if you're worried about me telling anyone, I won't, believe me. I mean it. I won't tell anyone," he said.

The Wine Cellar
A NOVELLA

To Michael and Frances

part ONE

i

He had never heard of Pearl Harbor. He knew nothing specific about the Japanese, only that they were Orientals and looked like Chinese. In his ignorance, which he now faced in himself with fear, he doubted that he had ever seen one. He listened to the old Zenith with the awareness of a man whose life had once before experienced the gross upheaval of war.

While the broadcaster's voice faltered in the description of the bombing, Bertocci remembered the prolonged disaster on the Italian front. He had been a private in the infantry then and the war, he felt, had made him less of a man. Now the disease was taking hold again. Who would suffer?

Ciro Bertocci had provided for his family conscientiously until a heart attack forced him to retire.

A few months before the attack his eldest son, Anthony, had been graduated from high school. There was talk of college, but the lack of money in the household had made enrollment impossible.

Bertocci had two unmarried daughters: thirty-year-old Angella and twenty-five-year-old Regina, each of whom had spent three years in high school without getting beyond the second year. When Angella quit school she took a job in a clothing factory where some years later, after she, too, left school, Regina also found work. For a while then, Bertocci thought that his financial condition would change for the better; but the income of the sisters was meager and what money they contributed to the household barely paid for the food they ate. Yet, before his heart attack, the father had managed to save money enough to send Anthony to night school, where he was now learning to become a toolmaker. It was not a university, but his eldest son would have a trade and would some day feel the dignity of being a craftsman. With this possibility the father was happy.

He listened to the details of the bombing, his head leaning to one side toward the speaker of the radio. It had started to snow, and as he listened he watched the flakes settle on the outside sash of the parlor window, strike against the glass and disappear. His family had not returned home from mass, and except for the presence of Robert, his twelve-year-old son who was somewhere in the house, he was alone.

Domenick Sardo, a short Sicilian with a dark, pointed face and suspicious little eyes, stood in the doorway of the parlor. Bertocci had heard him coming down the hall, and rather than listen to him talk while the radio was on, he reached over and turned the Zenith off. Sardo wore a black shabby overcoat that draped from his shoulders almost to his ankles. At the elbow of the right sleeve was a patch of faded brown cloth; and a large brass safety pin held the collar closed. Bertocci had known him for fifteen years and had never grown to like him. Domenick was the local shoemaker. Once there had been a scandal involving him with a deaf-mute girl of thirteen who, it was said, had been lured into the back room of his shop where he took advantage of her imbecility. A cursory investigation took place, but nothing was proved, since the girl was unable to relate the details of her experience clearly enough to have the shoemaker arrested. He was given a warning by the police and was told that it would go better for him in the future if the girl was not allowed to enter the shop. Bertocci, having got word of the incident from his wife, increased his dislike for the shoemaker and refused to do business with him. When it was necessary, against the advice of his wife, he took his shoes for repairs to a small shop located almost two miles across town.

The shoemaker stood anxiously in the doorway of the parlor, the snow melting on his coat and dripping onto the faded rug. He panted heavily and his hands shook as he unfastened the pin at the collar. He took off his coat, and after shaking it thoroughly, hung it over his arm. His hat remained on his head, and his small eyes looked furtively around the room.

"Ciro," he said, his breath quickening. "You have heard what has happened? It is going to be war!"

"I have heard," Bertocci said, his eyes downcast.

"Antonio," Domenick said, looking around the room, "he knows?"

"Yes," the father said.

"Roberto," the shoemaker said with forced concern, "he is fortunate he is too young."

"No one is fortunate," the father said in Italian. "We will all suffer."

"But there is nothing we can do, Ciro. For months I read in paper what is to come." The shoemaker paused, then he said emphatically in broken English, as if he had come suddenly upon a profound truth, "It is all politics." He stood in his wet shoes and his bony hand played with the rim of his hat.

Bertocci sat in his chair silently, hoping that Domenick would leave. He could not help feeling his distaste for the man increase, but he could not stop himself from agreeing with what he had just said, and he felt embarrassed.

"Maybe you are right, Domenick Sardo," he said, looking away. "It is all politics. There is nothing we can do."

"They will need many men, Ciro," the shoemaker said.

"They will find them."

"Your Antonio," the shoemaker said, pointing at Bertocci, "he is the age of my Angelo. They will go together, no?"

"There is time for them," Bertocci answered wearily.

The shoemaker fidgeted with his coat, draping it first over one arm and then the other. He hesitated now to move into the room, hoping that Bertocci would ask him to sit down and offer him a glass of wine in token of what he felt was a fate common to both their sons. But Bertocci said nothing. He sat impatiently while the shoemaker, still standing in the doorway of the parlor, played self-consciously with the rim of his hat. Slowly he moved into the room and stood cautiously in front of the silent Bertocci.

"Maybe there is not much time for them, Ciro," he said suddenly.

Bertocci looked up into Sardo's dark face, shifted again in his chair and then sighed with exasperation. "I am tired now," he said politely. "Please, you must go."

"But I have come to talk, Ciro," the shoemaker said, his hands flailing out in front of him.

"There is nothing we can talk about, Domenick Sardo."

"But my Angelo and your Antonio they must fight, Ciro."

Bertocci strained forward in his chair. "Antonio does not have to fight," he said loudly.

"But they will be the age soon," the shoemaker said.

He lifted his coat from one arm and slung it, disheveled, over the other. "I have figured it out," he continued excitedly. "In only ten months they will be old enough to fight in a war for their country."

With both arms, Bertocci lifted himself out of the chair; he felt the anger constrict the muscles in his face.

The shoemaker pulled himself back towards the door. "My Angelo," he muttered brokenly, "he will go proudly." He had just finished saying this when he felt the air being choked off at his throat.

They found their father lying across the threshold of the parlor. Anthony first listened for his heartbeat. When he felt it, he asked his sisters to lift the old man by the legs while he and Robert took him by the shoulders. Then slowly, together, they got him into bed, undressed him and called for the doctor.

The examination showed that he had experienced a mild heart attack. This, the doctor explained, was followed by a fainting spell, probably caused by overexertion and, he added, overexcitement. He gave two injections to Bertocci and told his wife, Philomena, that her husband was to be kept in bed for the next five days, during which time he would make another visit. He wrote out a prescription, tore it from his pad and handed it to her. "Give him one of these every four hours. If he gets any worse call me, but by all means do not let him out of bed until I see him again." The doctor put on his coat, closed his bag and stood in the doorway of the bedroom. "You should get the medicine as soon as possible and give it to him as soon as he wakes."

Anthony moved away from the bedside. "I'll get the

medicine," he said, and left the room. When he returned
with his coat on and his overshoes in his hand, the doctor
was waiting.

"I'll drive you to the drugstore, son. It's getting worse
outside and you'll have a hard enough time on your way
back anyway."

With this, Anthony started putting on his overshoes.
The wife, who had finished adjusting the bedclothes on
her husband, turned to the doctor. "How much will it be,
Doctor?" she asked.

"It will not be more than two dollars for the medicine,
I would judge."

"How much is it then for you to come here, Doctor?"
asked the wife again.

"It's three dollars for the visit and two dollars for the
injections." He paused, then he said, "But you don't have
to pay now if you don't have it."

"Now I have it," she said quickly. "Yes, Doctor, here."

She went to the bureau, opened the top drawer, took
out a round tin can and unscrewed its cover. When she
reached her hand in, there was the sound of loose change
against the tin, and the crinkling of old paper bills. The
doctor stood uneasily in the doorway waiting. She took
out all of the bills, placed the can on top of the bureau and
walked over to the bed. Some of the bills had been folded
individually. She began unfolding them one by one, laying them down on the bedspread beside her husband. She
counted out all of the paper money that had been in the
can. There were five one-dollar bills spread out side by
side on the bed.

"It is not enough," she said. She straightened up, went
back to the can and removed the change. Counting it out
into her palm, she found that she was thirty cents short.
She looked at the doctor.

"It's all right," he said nervously. "Really, you don't
have to." He turned towards the door.

"Wait, Doctor," she said. "I have it." She took Bertocci's trousers off the back of the chair. Searching the pockets, she finally found his black leather purse with its silver-ball latch. She fumbled with the latch. When the purse opened she emptied it quickly on the bed. "It is more than is needed," she said. She picked up all the money from the bed and handed five dollars to the doctor.

"There is really no need," he said uncomfortably. "You can pay when . . . "

"It is all right, Doctor. You take it," she broke in.

The doctor reached out, took the money reluctantly and picked up his bag. "It will be difficult driving now. Please," he said to Anthony, "I must go."

"Yes, Doctor," the mother said. "*Momento.*" She handed Anthony a five-dollar bill. "It will be enough now." She was breathing rapidly. "You come back quick," she said, smiling.

"All right," Anthony said, and with this, he stepped away quickly to catch up with the doctor, who had already left the room.

Anthony returned home with the medicine just after his father had waked up. He came into the room, his face reddened by the cold and with snow melting on the shoulders of his coat and packed tightly into the metal clasp of his overshoes. Stomping his feet first, he gave the medicine to his mother, who had been warning her husband not to get up. Bertocci refused to listen, trying strenuously to lift himself out of bed. Arguing loudly against this, she put the medicine on the chair and held him down on the bed by the shoulders. "*Aspetto,* Ciro," she said, "please." But Bertocci kicked his feet out from under the blankets and swung them over the side of the bed to the floor.

"This is not good," his wife said.

Bertocci fell back onto the bed. Exhausted, he let his wife and Anthony lift up his legs and put them under the bedclothes. After they finished covering him again, he remained silent with his eyes closed and his head sunk deep into the pillow.

His wife picked up the bottle of pills and shook one out onto her palm. "Water, Antonio," she said, and when Anthony returned with the glass full of water, she held out the pill to her husband.

"Take, Ciro," she said softly.

Bertocci looked at the pill and then at his wife. "What is this I should take?" he asked.

"It's the medicine I went for," Anthony said, his coat dripping with water. "The doctor was here," he added.

Bertocci raised his head. "Why the doctor?"

"Because you fainted. You had a heart attack. Like before," Anthony said.

Bertocci's wife held out the pill. "You must take this and stay quiet, Ciro."

"I do not need that."

His wife pleaded, "It is what the doctor has given."

"There is no reason you called for him."

"You were on the floor," Anthony said.

Bertocci looked at his wife. "Where does the money come from?"

"It is what little I had. The rest is from you."

Bertocci pounded his fist into the bedclothes. "It is a waste."

"It is not much for what the doctor has done."

"He has done nothing for me I say."

"He had to give you two injections," Anthony said. "And we had to buy the medicine too." He began taking off his coat.

Bertocci answered in Italian, "Medicine is useless for

me." He coughed and then asked, "How much did you pay?"

"It came to two dollars," Anthony said. "Exactly what the doctor said it would." He handed his mother the three dollar bills. She put them into the leather purse, snapped it closed and placed it on the chair.

"It is too much," Bertocci said.

His wife held out the pill again. "It is needed. Please, Ciro, take it."

"It will do no good."

"You have to take it," Anthony said.

"Please, Ciro."

"It is of no use to me," Bertocci said morosely. He began coughing deeply, spasmodically, and his eyes bulged open as he stared at the ceiling, his chest heaving under the bedclothes.

"Ciro, please," his wife cried.

He stopped coughing and after a while he said clearly, "I am all right."

"Yes, Ciro. You take," his wife pleaded.

Finally he reached out for the pill, took it and put it into his mouth. She placed her hand under his head, and as she raised it up a little she brought the glass of water to his lips. He drank quickly, swallowed once and then leaned back into the pillow with his eyes closed. After a while he opened them. "I will listen to the war now," he said. "Antonio, you will bring the radio in here."

After the radio was placed into position against the wall near the head of the bed, Anthony crawled under and plugged the line cord into the wall socket. Coming out from under the bed, he turned the switch on, and in a few seconds the voice of the broadcaster came through the static and filled the room. Bertocci leaned over and turned the volume down.

"I will be alone now," he said tiredly to his wife.

She looked forlornly at Anthony and he followed her out of the room.

ii

Sardo lived with his only son, Angelo. His wife, with whom Bertocci had always been on friendly terms (they were both Neopolitans and had come from the same village in Italy), had died after a prolonged struggle with pulmonary influenza. During the course of her illness Bertocci had attended her conscientiously with periodic visits. As the visits increased, he came to see the fortuitous and inconsiderate attitude with which the shoemaker regarded his wife's disease. Bertocci would sit beside her brass bed, and in a dialect foreign to her husband, speak to her quietly. Then, furtively and with mock curiosity, Domenick would look through the door of the sickroom, sneer at his wife and Bertocci, and disappear into the kitchen. He would never come into the room unless she called to him, his wife said. She said that she did not care. She said there was no time left to care, and that she would not live through the winter anyway and could not try to understand now why he acted as he did. She said that her life with him had been meaningless, and that she had continued with him for the sake of her son and her only fear now was that her son would become just like his father. There was nothing left. He would never change. She said that she did not care whether she lived or died.

But in her confinement she was not helpless. She was capable of administering medication to herself. She ate little and required only simple meals that Domenick prepared grudgingly; but during her illness she watched her household slip into abject filth, and it was this that bothered her. She was concerned mostly with the condition of her sickroom, and she pleaded with her husband to have it cleaned; but neither her husband nor Angelo, who appeared in the household only to eat and sleep, had made any attempt to gratify her wish. Bundles of old newspapers that Domenick had saved in the hope of selling them to the junkman had been tied with coarse yellow twine and thrown randomly against the walls; piles of loose clothing littered the floor, some of them unwashed and smelling sour; stale dinner plates of past meals were piled disreputably in a wicker chair, and dusty green quart bottles with wired porcelain stoppers that Domenick had bought in preparation for the wine he never made stood meaningless and naked in the corners; and everything in the room, mean and desolate under the ascetic glow from the one hanging bulb, was covered evenly with a sinister film of gray dust. Since the only window was never opened, the air in the small room was always heavy with the pungent scent of medicines and the smell of cooked garlic that wafted persis ently through the door from the adjoining kitchen.

If the ailing woman needed anything, such as more water in the blue glazed pitcher she kept on the little end table at the side of her bed, or if she became nauseated by the presence of her own excrement turning rank in the porcelain wash basin she used as a bedpan, her husband would balk at the simple requests that would have met her needs. Whenever he did enter the room, he moved around stealthily like a man walking on the edge of a pit. He would never speak, but his lips moved continually as if he were communicating with someone in the room other than his wife.

After the death of his wife, Domenick moved with Angelo into a musty three-room tenement flat that overlooked a bed of railroad tracks stretching behind the houses through a field of tangled weeds. This was the only tenement building in the neighborhood. Its small square

of land was adjacent to Bertocci's yard and was separated
from it by a picket fence. On Sundays, during the late
spring, Bertocci would often see the shoemaker moving
stoop-shouldered through the field searching for dandelions. Bertocci had a strong craving for the vegetable, but
since his first heart attack he did not have the strength to
go into the field and pick a few pounds for himself. Instead he would sit by the kitchen window and watch
Domenick forage among the weeds until he quit the field
with a sack of dandelions slung over his shoulder. When
Sardo was about to pass below the window, Bertocci
would call a greeting to him, hoping he would be given at
least a small portion of the vegetables out of which he
could make a salad, but the shoemaker would slink by
without looking up, turn the corner in silence, and disappear into his house.

"I spit in your blood," the old man would yell out in
Italian, and he would slam the window shut.

Once, while working in his small tomato garden that lay
in a narrow strip of yard alongside the house, Bertocci had
the feeling he was being watched. The shoemaker had
come quietly to the fence and was peering slyly over the
tops of the pickets. He did not speak. Bertocci did not
turn around; he paused a moment and then, kneeling on
the ground, went back to his work, tamping the black
earth against the base of the stems and retying the plants
that had come loose on their wooden stakes. When he had
accomplished this, all the while feeling Sardo's eyes following his movements, he meticulously picked about five
pounds of ripened tomatoes, wiped the film of dust from
each one and placed them carefully into the pouch of his
canvas apron. When Bertocci stood up, his apron bulging,
Domenick Sardo looked greedily at the red spheres, his
thin lips opening into a salutary smile, showing his un-
even yellow teeth. Bertocci deigned not to look into the
shoemaker's face. With his back to the fence, he began to

make his way out of the garden. Sardo took hold of the pickets in both of his fists. Raising his head cunningly over the fence as he watched the old man step clear of the plants, he called out quickly, *"Bène pomodori matura, Ciro."*

The old man looked down at the ground and then turned to face the shoemaker. "You have been watching me. Why?" he asked gravely.

"Because I see you have fine *pomodori*, Ciro."

"I have worked a long time for them."

"I have watched you, Ciro," the shoemaker said, smiling. He let go of one picket and scratched the side of his stubbled face. "I have no garden, Ciro. The yard is too small."

The old man looked away. He shifted his arms under the apron and then turned to face the Sicilian. "You have a big field, Domenick Sardo," he said loudly.

Domenick shuffled a few feet back from the fence, his hands flailing. "But I pick only a little dandelions. There are not many now, Ciro. They have made milk."

The old man cleared his throat. "I see what you pick, Domenick Sardo."

For a while neither man spoke. In the silence that fell between them Bertocci became increasingly aware of a disconcerting desire to give a tomato to the shoemaker, whose eyes moved nervously from the ground to the bulging apron. Finally, Bertocci stepped back into the garden.

"You will go to the field tomorrow?" he asked cautiously.

Domenick took hold of the pickets again. *"Si,* Ciro," he said, nodding his head. "It is Sunday. I go to the field."

Bertocci moved up close to the fence. He looked down into the pouch of his apron and began to study his tomatoes. To some of them were attached pieces of dried leaves. Other still had the ends of broken stems sticking out of them. He culled through the red globes until he found one that he liked. It was firm and delicately colored near the top with a translucent crystalline green. He raised it slowly in his palm. Sardo, filled with anticipation, looked eagerly at the vegetable glinting before his eyes. He reached over the pickets, his fingers spreading above the tomato. Bertocci, feeling a contradiction in what he was about to do to a man whom he hated openly, drew his hand away in fear, but again he experienced the pull of desire to follow through with his offer and face in himself the humility he knew the gesture would produce. He handed the tomato to the shoemaker. Sardo took hold of it, and as his eyes narrowed into a sinister squint, he pulled his hand back across the fence. The old man stood motionless watching him. Sardo fondled the tomato, looking at its size and its color critically; then, twisting off the bit of stem with the force of a man whose arrogance is implied in the motion, and without looking at Bertocci, he spun around and ran across the little yard into his house.

Bertocci stood quietly among his tomato plants. He was not surprised by what the Sicilian had done, and despite his humiliation and what he now felt to be self-hate coming over him, he managed a forlorn smile before leaving the garden.

That evening at the supper table he scornfully refused to eat the tomatoes his wife had prepared, and later, while lying in bed, he found himself mulling over the fact that he had given one to the shoemaker. It was dawn before he finally fell off to sleep.

The shoemaker knew little about Anthony's private life, but he still held for him a ceaseless envy. He had had his eye on him for a long time, ever since he was told that

Anthony had been graduated from high school, for Sardo's own son had left school after the eighth grade. Bertocci's wife had come into his shop on that June afternoon, and while waiting for Sardo to find a bag for her shoes, she elaborated proudly on her son's accomplishment. This news had produced in him such nausea that he closed his shop early—because of the heat, read the little sign on his door—and was unable to eat comfortably for two days. Now he looked with a sullen concern upon Anthony's effort to complete night school. He usually closed his shop a few hours after dusk, but if he felt the agonizing gloom settle over him, he would close early and then sit morosely behind the dusty window and wait until Anthony passed on his way to school, carrying his two thick manuals under his arm. Books had always impressed the shoemaker, and although he could read with only a negligible degree of comprehension, he had attempted once to read a volume of Wells' *Outline of History*. Before going to school one night, Anthony had come into the shop with a pair of shoes. While he was taking the shoes out of the bag to explain what he wanted done to them, the shoemaker fingered quickly through the pages of a machinist's manual that Anthony had placed on the counter. When the shoemaker saw the complicated graphs and the strange mathematical formulas on the pages, he closed the book disgustedly and sneered under his breath.

The next morning, however, after he had finished his meager breakfast, he had by chance seen a twenty-volume encyclopedia advertised on the back of a *True Adventure* magazine that Angelo had left opened on the kitchen table. That night, alone in his room, Domenick carefully read the instructions explaining how the books could be purchased. The first volume would cost five dollars—a sum that staggered him—but as he read on he became more curious. The two volumes of Wells', he found, were given free as a bonus offer, and the encyclopedia, except for the first volume, could be bought over a year's time on installment. He felt, as he read further, that the price of the first volume along with the two Wells' was worth the remaining books that could be his at half price. He removed the order coupon with a razor blade, filled in his name and then wrote in the name and address of his shop. In an envelope borrowed from a next door neighbor he enclosed a dirty five-dollar bill. The following morning he took the envelope from under his mattress where he had hidden it, and on his way to the shop, shoved it quickly into the mail box.

While Domenick Sardo waited for his books he found it difficult to concentrate on his work. Three customers who had been doing business with him since the day when he had first opened his shop refused to accept their shoes when they saw the faulty stitching along the edge of the soles. They demanded to have the work done over. Another woman who had had a high heel replaced while she waited, returned the next day with the heel broken off. Sardo examined the shoe and found that the nails had worked loose. When she refused to pay for the second replacement, he sneered spitefully under his breath. Realizing he needed her business, since she was new in the neighborhood, he let her have her way. After she left he shuffled despondently into the back room, where he stood in the shadows and pulled frantically at his hair. These two incidents and the fact that his business was failing, filled him with disgust. He cursed his life, and while he worked over his last, pounding it hatefully with his hammer, he swore aloud against the misery of his world.

But the Wells' was the first to arrive at the end of two weeks. After looking at the bulky package, turning it over in his hands and tapping it curiously with his knuckles, he placed it on his workbench and tore at the cardboard covering until he was able to fit his fingers into the opening he had made. The book slid out easily. He drew his palm across its shiny jacket, then raised it to his nose and sniffed. Immediately, the newness of the smell elated him. He put the book down and, mumbling to himself, began to finger through the pages. The absence of pictures at first dissatisfied him, but when the odor of quick type rose to his nostrils he was filled with the sudden awareness of an impending adventure, of the existence of a new and private world whose mysteries he was going to explore. He locked the door of his shop early and pulled the big green shade down over the plate glass window. Then he turned on the bulb over his workbench, and in the silence of his thoughts he began to read.

When there were no customers in the shop, Domenick would sit on his wooden stool with his new book held open under the counter where it could not be seen. He would read slowly, forcing himself through each sentence. When he was not reading, he kept the book hidden out of sight in the drawer of an old roll-top desk located in the back room. If he had the urge to read at home, he would deftly wrap the book in brown paper, stuff it under his coat and try to get to his house without the book being seen.

He managed to read a little each day, grappling desperately for the gist of esoteric words and the meanings of the complicated sentences they created. Finally, after three months of an agonizing struggle in which he had labored through only the first chapter, he flung the book aside in disgust and never opened it again. The shoemaker began to realize after this that his life would go on without change. In his attempt to read the book he had not seen so much as a shadow of the world he had expected to see. Yet, even in his anger and frustration, books continued to fascinate him, and the people who read them, remote as he now felt them to be, produced in him an acute, helpless rage.

iii

Anthony's fair complexion, blue eyes and darkening blond hair were features common to the northern regions of Italy where Bertocci's ancestors had once lived. In time, and in spite of his wife's conviction that he should spend his spare time equally with all of his children, the father gradually came to favor the company of his eldest son. As a child, Anthony was the sole member of the family taken to the Italian market in the city when certain foods were unavailable in the neighborhood groceries. He was taken on walks through the park that was situated a few blocks from the house. By the time Anthony was fifteen years old, the father had taught him to use the single-barrel shotgun that had been given to him by a distant relative whose eyesight had failed in his later years. Together, with food put up the night before, they would start out on a Saturday morning, take the trolley car to the end of the line and from there walk some two miles to the deep woods where they would hunt for rabbits.

Anthony had always shown a willingness to obey Bertocci, yet by the time he turned seventeen he had developed an interest in football and—against his father's wishes—had won a position on his high school team. Fearing injury to the boy, the father had periodically warned him not to play, threatening severe punishment if he did. But the boy continued to play secretly, and after graduation joined a local team. One Saturday a few months before his second heart attack, Bertocci while having his hair cut, overheard a conversation about his son's accomplishments in a game played the day before. Returning home from the barbershop in near rage, he found the boy's playing equipment in a duffle bag hidden in the cellar, brought the bag up into the kitchen and dumped the pieces out on the floor. His wife was preparing supper at the stove and his eldest daughter was beginning to set the table. After ordering the daughter out of the room, Bertocci, sitting pensively at the table, waited for his son to come home. From time to time he glanced uneasily at the clock on the kitchen wall, and at ten minutes past five o'clock, ten minutes past the precise hour when the family ate their final meal of the day, he got up from his chair and began pacing the floor. There was a contemplative look on his drawn face. His wife, who argued against his decision that no one would eat until the boy was punished, left her stove in disgust.

Alone now in the steaming kitchen, Bertocci culled through the playing equipment in the duffle bag. In its hardness and in its texture, and especially in its purpose, which he could surmise only from the various shapes, the pieces were totally foreign to him. Curiously he examined the shoulder pads, the hip guards, the orange and black jersey which he held out in front of him by the sleeves, with its huge block number ninety-five in glaring white sewn perfectly to the front and back of the shiny cloth. He scrutinized one of the shoes, running his fingers over the clusters of rubber cleats screwed to the soles. He shook his head in bewilderment, and let the shoe drop to the pile at his feet. In a while, standing quietly above the equipment, he lowered his head and his eyes narrowed into an intense stare, the kind of punishment he would give the boy suddenly came to him.

Anthony came through the kitchen doorway and halted

before his waiting father, who stood holding the packed duffle bag on the floor in front of him. Their eyes met instantly. Bertocci handed the bag to his son, and in a voice that rose slightly above a whisper, said, "You will come with me into the cellar, Antonio." Without saying a word, Anthony let his father pass through the kitchen doorway. Morosely the boy followed him down into the cellar.

Robert, whose chore it was to tend the furnace on weekends, was called by Bertocci from the bottom of the cellar stairs. When the wife answered instead, asking what was taking place, Bertocci stomped back up into the house, found Robert and told him to stoke the furnace in preparation of what would now be an example also for him. The boy, in his reluctance to take part in what he knew would be punishment for his brother, felt a stubborn resistance to obey the father. With a shyness that irritated Bertocci he looked down at the floor and refused to take hold of the poker as he was told. Taking him by the shoulders, Bertocci led him up to the furnace and opened the furnace door. The three of them stood like silhouettes in the dim glare of the bulb hanging from the overhead beam behind them. The fire light played across their solemn faces and reached beyond them to play on the granite stones of the foundation wall. Under his father's directions now, Robert, trembling, took hold of the poker and stared into the blue and yellow flames sputtering out of the bed of hot coals. He hesitated with the poker's tip poised before the open furnace. When his father tapped him on the shoulder, the boy, filled with remorse, jabbed the poker into the banked coals. Feeling the presence of his brother behind him, Robert worked rapidly, and when the fire was stoked to his father's approval he stepped back with tears in his eyes, glanced at Anthony helplessly and lowered his head.

Without being told, Anthony gripped the drawstring of the duffle bag, looked at his silent father and opened the bag. Taking the pieces out one by one he threw them into the furnace, and when the bag was empty, it too was thrown into the fire. For what seemed a long time, during which Anthony could feel the anger mounting in him, the three watched the mantle of flames eat at the leather, at the jersey and at the crumbling canvas bag—all of which disappeared in a roil of smoke. Bertocci then, with his jaw set hard, closed the furnace door and went up into the kitchen to eat. In silence the two boys followed.

Supper was eaten in silence. Robert, having eaten little of his food, left the table and went to his room. The next morning at breakfast he was gone.

Although he did not show it, Bertocci reasoned regretfully that his son was no longer in the house because of the humiliation that he had suffered. After looking into the boy's room, the wife told her husband that Robert had taken some clothing with him and that the imitation sharkskin suitcase that had for years sat unused in a closet was gone. She stood over Bertocci, who went on with his meal and finished it. Without so much as a nod to her supplication that they tell the police of their son's having run away, he got up from the table, went into the parlor and dozed off in his chair.

During the previous night Anthony had felt a deep but temporary hatred toward Bertocci. Standing now in the doorway of the parlor and staring intently at him, he felt only an inexpressible curiosity. Bertocci stirred once, rolled his head to the side on the back of the chair and thrust out his legs. He did not wake. Beside him Anthony could see the Zenith with its volume turned down; its dial light glowed from its tarnished mahogany face and a low, steady hum from the speaker rippled under the silence of the room. He stared at his father's left hand slung down from the armrest near the radio. The other lay still on the rest nearest him; he could make out the network of thick veins on the back of the hand, the worn fingernails, the dulled, yellowing patina in the grain of the nails and the hair that grew down beyond the tawny knuckles almost to the ends of the fingers in little isolated swirls. His eyes now followed the thick line of the arm up to the shoulders beneath the wool of the coat sweater, as coarse as the hair on his hands, and the swirls of hair that showed on the short neck below the gray stubble on his chin. As he studied the face he could not believe the mystery he saw: the eyes rounded full under their closed lids; the lined forehead above them with its thick dark brows; the thick, quiet lips partly opened; the wide nose; the high cheekbones; the wholeness of the head now taking on proportions so awesome in sleep that Anthony was afraid to move lest it come to life from that world of silence, wake and lift itself out of the shadows of the room and suddenly speak. He is my father, he heard, and Bertocci stirred again and shifted in his chair. The son wanted to reach out now and touch the sleeping hand, and he could feel the desire to do it as surely as he could feel the trembling of his own hand. My father, he heard again, and he saw his face as he had seen it in the light coming from the furnace door. My father, he heard once more, and it was his own voice talking inside of him, telling him to reach, even against the fear that held him back and finally drew him out of the room.

If the weather had not been stormy on the night he had left home, Robert would have made it to the elevated train station less than a mile away and from there to the city, where he planned to take a bus. Where he would go he did not know, but as he moved through the mounting drifts in the deserted streets and felt the wind bite his face, he decided to go back to his father's house and spend the night in the cellar, resolving that in the morning he would start out again from there. On the way back to the house then, the shoemaker, who had watched the boy pass by some minutes before, saw him pass again below his window. In seconds Domenick Sardo appeared half-dressed on the stoop, called excitedly to the boy through the wind and invited him to stay for the night.

The small room in Sardo's apartment faced the stretch of land that separated the two houses. Through its only window Robert could see across to the lighted parlor windows of his own house. Along one wall of the room stood a narrow iron bed with a sunken mattress, a stained, lifeless pillow lay on the floor beside it. Sardo, smiling quickly, picked up the pillow, punched it into shape, and placed it carefully on one end of the mattress.

"It will be comfortable, Roberto," he said. "And I have blankets for you, yes."

Robert sat down on the edge of the bed while the shoemaker, who had run out of the room, returned with two woolen blankets folded neatly one on top of the other.

"The door I will leave open to let in the heat," he said.

Now in his silence and in the uneasiness that came over him, Robert felt the austerity of the room with its curtainless window and its bare plaster walls that were cracked in some places to the exposed wooden laths. Along the baseboards were holes stuffed with rags. In the far corner near the door, sitting on a wooden crate, an unshaded lamp glowed dimly and sheets of dusty newspapers lay scattered on the cracked linoleum floor. But it was not only the austerity of the room that disturbed the boy. It was also the closeness of Domenick Sardo on the bed beside him, with his polite falsities, his pointed face, his small shifting eyes and inquiring mood that brought on with sudden fear Robert's desire to leave. Sensing the boy's uneasiness and even his wish to leave, Sardo got up quickly and left the room again. He returned this time with a dish of cold meat, a half-loaf of bread and a glass of wine.

"Eat," the shoemaker said with a sudden grin. He held the dish of meat in one hand, with the glass of wine nestled in between the meat and the loaf of bread in the other. "Your father," he asked softly, "he has sent you away?"

Robert shook his head. "No," he said quietly, and in a trembling voice went on to tell the shoemaker what Bertocci had forced him to do.

As if he did not hear, Sardo placed the food on the blankets and sat down, placing his arm around the boy's shoulder. "You will be all right here," he said.

The boy could feel the heat of the bony arm on the back of his neck. He pulled away nervously and stared at the floor.

The shoemaker laughed quietly, as if surprised. "You are afraid of me?" he asked.

"No," Robert answered. He glanced at the food. "I'm just not hungry."

"The wine then," the shoemaker said, sliding his arm from the boy's neck. "It will help you to sleep, Roberto."

The boy said nothing. He wanted to get up and leave the house, but now the weight of the trembling hand moving along his thigh held him fixed in place. When Robert thought he could bear the hand no longer, the shoemaker suddenly got up, smiled and took in a breath.

"Roberto," he said, "you sleep and tomorrow we will talk. You will feel better then. No?" But Domenick Sardo did not wait for an answer. He picked up his food and hurried out of the room.

Torn now between his desire to leave the house of

Domenick Sardo and the necessity to stay, the boy moved to the window of the small room and stood looking out into the storm across the space of the yard into the darkened windows of his father's house. He mused on the streaks of ice that had collected along the clapboards reflecting the glare of a street lamp through the tumult of snow. He listened to the wind. He heard it wheeze in the chinks of the room. He heard the gusts of it rise and diminish and rise again to rattle the window in its frame. Presently he thought of his father sleeping beyond the space between the houses that separated them. He thought of him somewhere lying in darkness beyond the snow; somewhere beyond the drone of the wind. He is my father, he said, and he said this inside of himself and stepped back into the shadows of the room and stood trembling with a fear whose cause he could not put into words. He went to the door and closed it. He turned off the lamp and got into bed. Fixing the blankets over himself he lay down and tried to sleep. In a while, sleep began to take him and the image of Bertocci's face receded in the darkness behind his eyes. In the morning when he woke, he still could not bring himself to leave this house despite his fear of Domenick Sardo.

iv

It was some three hours before noon when Domenick Sardo finished shoveling a path through the snow that had fallen the night before. The path led from the stoop of his house to the sidewalk, and he stood leaning on the handle of his shovel, looking out at the drifts that lay in the unplowed street. Bertocci, who had wakened from his early nap filled with irritation, had seen Robert briefly at the shoemaker's window. In a sudden rage he put on his coat and went out to face the Sicilian. Approaching him from the rear, he stopped an arm's length away, took out his handkerchief and blew his nose. The Sicilian turned quickly and stared at Bertocci, a wide suspicious grin showed on his lean face.

"*Buon giorno,*" he said, drawing back a step. "It is clean snow, no?"

"It is as snow should be, Domenick Sardo," Bertocci answered, folding the handkerchief carefully, first into one palm and then into the other.

The shoemaker looked away, gripped the shovel fiercely and heaved a cloud of snow into the street.

"You will send my son home," Bertocci said. He stood with his hands at his side now, working the fingers into a fist.

The Sicilian continued to shovel with his back lowered over the snow and his overcoat flapping open with each swing of his arms. He did not answer. Bertocci moved clear of the working shovel.

"I say to you for the last time, Domenick Sardo, you will send my Roberto home."

The shoemaker looked up at Bertocci. "The boy, he comes with his suitcase. So . . . I let him stay."

"I say you will send him home."

The shoemaker looked to his side and spit into the snow. Wiping his mouth with the back of his hand, he turned back to Bertocci. "It is enough," he said sarcastically, "that maybe you make him do things that he does not want to do. No?"

Bertocci coughed up a gout of phlegm, drew back his head and spit into the shoemaker's face. "It is enough maybe that I should kill you," he said in Italian.

The shoemaker stood calmly in place while the saliva ran down the side of his cheek. Bertocci, who felt a sudden shame come over him, waited for the Sicilian to wipe off the spittle, but Sardo stood with the smile widening on his lips, staring blankly into Bertocci's eyes. Bertocci then took out his handkerchief and handed the cloth to the grinning Sicilian.

"You will clean your face, Domenick Sardo," he said apologetically.

The shoemaker said nothing. Bertocci offered the handkerchief a second time but the Sicilian, shaking his head from side to side, refused. With his smile broadening contemptuously, he stepped back, raised his hand and stuck his finger into his nostril in a gesture of cleaning his nose. Bertocci felt the anger swelling in him. "I am a man who is wise to you, Domenick Sardo," he said, his breath quickening in his throat. "If my Roberto is not home before the hour, I will come for you with a knife." With this he threw the handkerchief at the shoemaker's feet, ground it into the snow with his heel, mumbled an obscenity in Italian, turned and walked back toward his house. At the gate leading into the front yard he stopped and, looking back, saw the Sicilian standing quietly in the snow with the shovel held at his side. He was still smiling and the spittle was still on his face.

In less than an hour after Bertocci had warned the shoemaker, Robert returned home. Angella was preparing the kitchen table for the afternoon meal. She was a large round girl with heavy breasts and thick fatty arms. Her jet-black hair was tied back in a tight bun. She turned when she heard her brother come through the kitchen doorway.

Angella Bertocci had always seemed on the edge of brooding thought, and except for occasional quiet laughter at the supper table or a sudden show of anger whenever a mistake in a dress she was sewing drew her out of her solitude, she was a girl who rarely expressed an emotion. When not at work she moved about the house or yard in one or another of her black dresses, invaded, it seemed, by somber preoccupations. Bertocci, who had always looked upon her as one whose life held limited possibilities, gave her little attention. But once a change had come over her that caused the father and the family to consider her with an interest they never before had felt. It all started a year ago, some two weeks after her thirtieth birthday, when a door-to-door shoe salesman drew up a chair next to her on the porch and began showing his wares displayed in a large flat catalogue held open on his knees. He had thick, dark eyebrows and slick, straight black hair that was combed into a tuft at the back of his head. The girl listened to him with the attention of a child and, after he finished his talk on the various styles from which she should make her choice, she told him her size and signed for three pairs of shoes.

A week went by before he called on her again. During the interim, Angella Bertocci drifted into a happy daze. Her dress became pampered and the low-heeled, dull black shoes she usually wore were given up for one of the three pairs of patent leather shoes that had come in the mail. She wore her bright new cotton print dresses too, and whenever she went for a walk in the nearby park among the oak trees and on the small paths that wound through solitary alders, she wore her new red pleated coat with its gold buttons down the front. During these walks, which increased from day to day, her thoughts of herself against the golden brown colors of the trees filled her with happiness, and the sound of the leaves shuffling beneath her new shoes elated her. She would stay out of doors for hours at a time. She was the last to come to the supper table, where the family, before taking any food, would wait curiously for her appearance. It seemed that her world had changed overnight. Her black hair, which had always been tied back in a bun or made into a braid that hung down her back, had been let out and now fell over her shoulders in long, soft furls. Even her features took on a particular quiet charm and there was in her deportment a relaxed quality of joy that seemed to touch them all. Unable to hold back the feelings he had over his daughter's transformation, Bertocci, one evening at supper, looked across the table directly into her eyes and in a quiet voice told her in Italian she was beautiful, as beautiful as an opening flower.

After Anthony's birth Bertocci had looked upon his daughters as necessary only because they contributed money to the household, and although he was never deliberately cruel to anyone in the family, he treated them as a man might treat a guest in the politely casual yet unfriendly atmosphere of a boarding house. He did allow them, after they had begged him for it, a small room at the rear of the house. He gave it to them on condition they pay for the material to make it livable, including the kerosene that burned now every night in the two-burner stove they used to heat the drafty room. The father had bought it at auction, not grudgingly but cautiously, repaired it himself, and put it in their room. He then told them specifically that they would from that time on pay for any repairs the stove might need. Sometimes the burners would fail to light properly, filling the room with smoke, and once, in their fear of freezing in a sudden cold spell, the sisters had bought a set of wicks that they installed themselves. When the valves were turned on, the burners flooded and, after they were lit, flamed up rapidly and overheated the stove and its oil supply tank in the rear. The father was called, and he shut off the burners before the heat ignited the supply tank, which had come dangerously close to exploding. He yelled at both daughters but he struck Angella with a blow that stunned her. She fell against the wall with her nose bleeding. As he continued to beat her, the girl screamed painfully. Bertocci, too, swore loudly as his hand fell repeatedly upon her head and face. Finally, the wife, who heard the cries from the kitchen, ran into the room and pulled her husband away from their daughter, who was sinking down unconscious against the wall.

This was the first time Bertocci had been driven to beat one of his children. At first, he had felt no guilt or shame for what he had done. His first concern was for the house. He had even refused to call a doctor for his daughter, whose nose continued to bleed slightly for almost an hour after she had been beaten. He then became worried, but his wife wrapped some crushed ice in a towel and applied it to the girl's nose. After a while the bleeding stopped and despite his relief, Bertocci was overcome by remorse. That night he was unable to sleep; the moaning of his daughter, lying awake in the dark of her unheated room, produced in him a feeling of inexpressible sorrow— whether for himself or for her, he did not know. Throughout that night in the dark of his own room, he listened to the sound of the wind against the rattling windows and against the loose clapboards of the house. By morning he swore he would never beat his children again.

On the Saturday following their first meeting, then, the salesman, as he had promised, came again. Without taking his eyes from the girl's lowered face he complimented her on her pleated coat and commented amiably on her new shoes and asked if they were comfortable. Showing him with her smile that they were, the girl had thought of asking his name, but the closeness of his face, the scent of pomade coming from his slicked hair, the sight of his white, starched collar glaring in the sunlight and the red silk tie visible between the wide lapels of his top coat silenced her words before she could say them aloud.

When he showed her the catalogue of winter footwear, explaining the various styles and the different qualities of each, she listened wih a shy look on her round face, nodding her head in agreement to whatever he said. By the time he handed her the order forms she had already made her choice: a pair of rubber snow boots and fleece-lined black rubber overshoes with zippers running up the sides. With the forms signed and in his briefcase, the man stood up, took her hand and kissed it, telling her he would visit again in a week.

The next Saturday the girl waited patiently on the front porch but the man never appeared, and at dusk on that day Angella Bertocci had gone back into the house filled with a pervading gloom. Her face, with her eyes downcast, expressed the realization that she would perhaps never see the man again.

A few days after this, while rummaging through the girls' room looking for a misplaced hammer, Bertocci found all of the footwear hidden under his daughter's bed. Like his wife he came to feel that Angella had been cajoled into buying them. He swore in a rage against what he believed to be his daughter's waste of money. His wife became fearful. She begged him not to concern himself with Angella's business. To this Bertocci had made no reply. He sat with his cheeks in his hands mumbling to himself at the kitchen table, and during supper in a loud steady voice reviled the salesman and suggested that Angella was a fool. He had forbidden her to leave the table while he talked. The girl had come near to crying and sat trembling in her chair. That night, while lying awake in her bed long into the morning, it came to her that her love for the man was stronger than all of the evil attributed to him by her father. In her desire to see him again she had continued for some three weeks after this to sit forlornly on the front porch waiting for his appearance.

But the man never appeared again. Certain now that he

had gone away for good, Bertocci became aggravated by his daughter's weekly vigils. He was moved, too, by an acute sense of concern. He could see the lack of color in her drawn face and mulled over her moody insistence to be left alone. In her apprehension, the wife felt that her daughter would become incurably heartbroken. Already she had missed three days of work in one week. What they could do about this they did not know. What they should do about their daughter's unhappiness they could not comprehend. So they simply watched as Angella Bertocci sunk gradually into prolonged, listless moods of self-pity in which she neither spoke, nor out of which she could draw the slightest appetite for food. One day, sitting across from her at the kitchen table, Bertocci explained to her that it was not good to miss any more work, for the money was needed to feed them. As important as this was, he said in Italian, choosing his words carefully, it was not good to let the heart punish itself for the mistakes of its own reason. He spoke quietly and placed his hand on hers. Although the footwear was a reminder of that mistake, he went on calmly, it was not so grave a mistake that it should cause her any more pain. He waited for the girl to speak but she seemed not to hear. Tears began to show in her eyes and Bertocci, growing uneasy in the face of his daughter's sentiments, was unable to find words to console her.

For almost three months after their talk, Angella Bertocci had gone to mass every morning and received holy communion. She lit candles too, but for what purpose she did not know. When not at work she spent most of her time sitting by the window of her room, her gaze lost among the leaves of the elm tree that grew in the yard in back of the house. She gave up wearing her new cotton print dresses and wore now, as she had in the past, her hand-knitted shawls and the simply made black cotton dresses that hung loosely from her round shoulders. Her hair was again tied into a bun. An absent, almost hopeless stare seemed always to be in her eyes and in time, despite the concerns of her family, she began to live an existence so narrow that Bertocci all but forgot about her in his indifference.

Robert said nothing to his sister. He went on through the kitchen and into his room, put the suitcase on his bed and began taking out his clothes. His face had a look of solemn preoccupation. His eyes seemed shaded as if dulled by a weakening of light. Behind him, standing with her hands on her hips, Angella watched in silence, nodding her head as the boy arranged the clothes on the bed. He closed the suitcase and put it back into the closet. When he turned to his sister standing in the doorway of the room, she stared intensely at him and her scornful grin seemed to give certainty to his belief that he had done something wrong.

"Maybe you would like to live with the shoemaker," she said.

Robert said nothing. He made his way toward the doorway. With her hands on her hips, Angella blocked his way.

"Maybe he has a girl for you, Roberto. You would like that, no? A girl all to yourself to play with?" She broke into laughter and ran her fingers through her brother's hair.

"Let me by," Robert said.

"One of Domenick Sardo's, who cannot speak?" Her laugh was subtle now. "Did he tell you he knows of such girls? Roberto Bertocci? Look at me." She lowered her voice now. "She would like your curly hair? And your brown eyes? No?"

The boy could feel the anger mounting in him and he

blurted the words into her face. "You have shoes you don't even wear," he said. "And you look at them every night in your room." With this he pushed his way past his sister and ran into the adjoining room. His fear now was of his father, whom he had yet to face.

The father remained silent during the meal. With his fork held above his plate, he would look up, stare momentarily at Robert and quietly resume his eating. Periodically, Angella would stare at her brother, and the look in her eyes told him that she had not forgotten the remark he had made about her unworn shoes. From time to time, Philomena Bertocci got up from her chair and moved nervously from the table to the stove and back to the table, wondering how her husband would punish her son for having run away. Earlier she had begged him to forget the incident but, as if he were deaf to her words, he sat moodily in his easy chair without answering. Disgusted, she had sworn under her breath in Italian and left him sitting alone in the shadows of the room. Now the meal was finished and the daughters began clearing the table. Suddenly Bertocci spoke, and although his voice was firm, he spoke without anger. He ordered Robert to stay in his chair and told the others, including his wife, to leave the room.

With his eyes lowered now, he took out his handkerchief and wiped his mouth. Folding the handkerchief slowly, he placed it on the table beside him. He looked across at the boy, who sat mournfully watching. For a while nothing was said between them. The boy shifted in his chair and, as his father was about to speak, he blurted out his words, barely intelligible and, it seemed to Bertocci, without reason. "I . . . didn't want him . . . to touch me," he said.

He sat rigid as wood and looked across at Bertocci's solemn face. Then his eyes watched the quiet hands placed on top of one another, and his gaze, for it was a long and unblinking gaze now, traveled to his father's eyes and held them fixed as one would hold the eyes of a judge. Bertocci rubbed the stubble on his chin. He placed his hands again one on top of the other and sat calmly looking at the boy. Finally he spoke and his voice was again without anger.

"You are telling me, Roberto, that Domenick Sardo has put his hands on you?"

The boy lowered his head. "Yes," he said softly.

"And his hands touched you where?"

Bertocci waited. When he saw that the boy would not speak, he took in a breath, let it out slowly and continued. "You will not be afraid, Roberto. Where did his hands touch you? Speak, I say."

"I . . . don't . . . know," the boy said in a half whisper.

"Is it that you forget?"

"No."

Bertocci fell silent and after a moment he said with deliberate calmness, "You will think about what you want to say, Roberto, and when you know, you will tell me what it is. If you decide there is nothing to know then you will say nothing and there will be nothing that I should do to Domenick Sardo."

After a while, when he felt his fear diminish, the boy forced himself to speak, and in a faltering voice he told what the shoemaker had done. He raised his head, stared across at his father and waited. Bertocci got up from his chair, walked around to the other side of the table and placed his hand on Roberto's shoulder. "It is all right, Roberto," he said with relief, smiling. "It is all right because there is nothing I must do.

Turning slowly away, he went into the parlor. Finding

the rest of his family sitting with expectant looks on their solemn faces, he asked to be left alone. After they were gone he sat down in his chair, reached over and turned on the Zenith. In a few seconds the sound of a broadcaster's voice came through the silence of the room. Bertocci, with a smile coming to his lips, closed his eyes, listened a moment, felt the comfort of his chair and in a while was asleep.

part TWO

V

On Monday, December 8, 1941, the day after Bertocci's heart attack, war was declared. He listened every day to the Zenith, half in confusion and half in a state of wary concern for his family. He became irate at the idea of conflict, and on the weekend, after he was allowed out of bed, he suffered another mild attack while speaking to his family on the absurdity of war. He was returned to his bed and under orders from the doctor was told to remain quiet, with the radio turned off. The doctor, on second thought, said it would be better for him if he were taken to the city hospital, but Bertocci refused vehemently to be moved out of the house for any reason. He would rather pay the doctor his fee, he declared, than go to the city hospital free of charge. It was explained that his recent attack had left him with a mild form of angina, but even in its mild form it required bed rest and no excitement.

Bertocci was put on medication to help lessen the symptoms of the angina and at the same time to calm him down. The doctor would not say how long he would keep Bertocci in bed. It would depend upon his willingness to take medication and upon his effort to accept the situation of war as a condition he could not change.

So Bertocci remained in bed, listening intensely to each report on the course of the war. He grew increasingly concerned with the names of unfamiliar Pacific islands involved in the conflict, their locations and their characteristics. As to what real value they had ever had for the Americans or for the Japanese before the war, he could not understand, neither from the radio reports nor from the world history book and atlas, which Anthony had gotten for him from the public library. Now, whenever he heard the name of an island mentioned for the first time, he would locate it on the map and circle it with a red crayon. By the end of the winter he became familiar with the Japanese campaign to the point where he could predict their next move.

At first he knew little about the people of Japan as they were described to him by Anthony from the history book, but by the middle of spring—and contrary to what he had learned from the radio and newspapers—he had gained enough knowledge of their way of life to enable him to see that the facts of their existence were not too different from his own.

Still he could see no reason for the carnage, as he called it in Italian, and when reports started to be published disclosing the atrocities the Japanese were inflicting upon captured American prisoners, he knew it would be a war in which the same atrocities would be committed by the Americans in their retaliation. When he predicted to his family after the fall of Corregidor in May that the absurdity of the carnage would continue in favor of the Japanese maybe for the next two years, he became forlorn. There would be much suffering and death, he thought. He began to feel hopeless—a man whose reason could not in the least way affect the outcome or the pattern of the turmoil as he listened to its development from his sickbed.

Bertocci knew, and this began to worry him, that many men would now be killed in gaining back the islands that had been lost to the Japanese during the first eight months of the war. In his uncertainty as to the ultimate purpose—if there was one—for which they would die, he wondered if his son would be part of the campaign the Americans were certain to initiate in their attempt to regain their position in the Pacific. He realized the importance the navy would have in such an offensive. Because he knew his son preferred the navy over the army, he now spent his days aggravated by a persistent fear: he became upset to the point of swearing when Anthony told him he'd rather join the navy by his own choice than wait until he was drafted into the army.

Sometimes they would argue until the father became short of breath, coughing miserably. Anthony would ask him not to get excited, or Philomena, who usually heard the discussions from the kitchen, would come in and ask Anthony to leave the room. As the war intensified near the end of August, Anthony would more and more make slight references to the reasons he should leave night school and join the navy. Finally he said directly that since he would be drafted on his next birthday—the last day in October—he should be allowed to join the navy before the army took him. This had enraged the father, who refused then to listen to his son's arguments. Again, one Saturday afternoon in early September, Anthony made the decision not to attend school. He, along with his classmates, he told his father, would join the navy the following Monday morning, provided they passed the physical examination and their parents signed the permission forms. In any case, he went on, if his father did not sign for him, he would quit school and take a job in the local arsenal until he was drafted.

The intense discussion that developed this time caused Bertocci to experience a coughing spell aggravated by severe heart palpitations. When this condition did not lessen, during which time the wretched coughs were interspersed by loud swearing, Robert was sent to call for the doctor.

"I will sign nothing," the father yelled, and while they waited for the doctor he labored to breathe through the lulls in his coughs. By the time the doctor arrived he had calmed down, but still he swore that he would never sign. The doctor explained to him that if his excitement continued he would perhaps have a serious attack that would lay him up for good. He was given a sedative and told to rest.

"We are all upset these days," the doctor said.

"It is my son," Bertocci said.

"I know you're concerned, but there is little you can do." The doctor closed his bag. "Is he of age?" he asked Philomena Bertocci.

"It is his birthday on the last day of October. Yes," the mother said. She pressed her palms together, and then she went on, "But we pray every day that it will end and he will not have to go."

The doctor lifted his bag and moved towards the door. "Perhaps the worst will be over by then," he said, stopping at the door.

"It will get worse," Bertocci called from the bed.

"There is absolutely nothing we can do," said the doctor.

"I will not sign for him."

"He'll be drafted anyway whether you sign or not. You must realize this for your own good," the doctor said.

"I will not sign."

"You should rest now. Perhaps in a few days you can start to get up. A little each day."

"I am all right now," Bertocci said.

"Yes, but I will see you first in a few days before you get up. Tuesday we will see," the doctor said. He turned away slowly and left the room.

The father knew he could not prevent the drafting of his son, nor could he change his son's mind, which was made up definitely to join the navy. Yet he held to his conviction not to sign the permission forms even in the face of Anthony's argument that he'd be drafted anyway. At first he was disconcerted by his son's refusal to continue school. Then, a few days later, he came to realize that Anthony's schooling was a waste of money if he could not finish the course. With his own meager increase in savings —his daughters worked overtime now and contributed a little more for their room and board—the family could always use whatever money Anthony would give to the household. Yes, he thought, the extra money could go into repairs on the house.

Anthony continued to argue his point even after he had quit night school. He wagered persistently day after day that he'd be safer in the war as a sailor. The father answered him by saying he'd be safer at home away from the war, and that he'd be kept at home until the last minute of the final hour when they would have to come and take him away. With this, Bertocci said he wanted to hear no more. "It is enough, Antonio," the father said finally. "You will work until your birthday. Maybe we will see then what is to happen."

Anthony worked at the arsenal, hoping all the while his father would change his mind before his birthday. Most of his friends from night school had joined the navy. He heard, too, that Angelo Sardo had joined the marines and was waiting to be called for duty. Anthony looked upon this news as an insult to himself. He spoke little to his father, who seemed always under the burden of heavy thought as he moved about the household or sat in his wicker chair beneath the elm in back of the house. While in the house he would not listen to the Zenith, nor did he ask any of them to read to him from the newspapers. At night, before going to bed, he would sit alone for long periods in his armchair in the darkened parlor. He rarely spoke of the war, but once, while sitting in his wicker chair, he overheard two neighbors talking about a recent naval battle near an island called Guadalcanal. He had difficulty pronouncing the island's name and looked upon the defeat as more carnage.

"It's in the Solomons," Anthony said, and went back to his food.

"I know of the Solomon Islands. What has happened today I do not know about," the father said.

Anthony looked across at him again. "The Japs have been trying to take Guadalcanal," he said with some uneasiness. He hesitated, then added, "We've stopped their invasion."

"I have heard today that a ship has sunk. Is it so?" The father waited for an answer. Anthony turned away, and Bertocci spoke again. "Is it true? There is a ship sunk, Antonio?"

Anthony put down his fork. "It's true," he said. "We lost the aircraft carrier *Wasp* yesterday."

The father lowered his voice. "It has gone down then?"

"Yes," Anthony said. "Off Guadalcanal."

"It is unfortunate," Bertocci said in Italian.

Anthony raised his voice now. "It didn't have a chance," he said.

"It is no difference, Antonio."

"It does make a difference," the son replied.

The father went back to his eating. "Maybe it is so," he said, and he went on to finish his meal without speaking again.

Bertocci kept to himself most of the time. If he remained inside the house, he would usually spend his time in the cellar, sitting on a wooden stool in an unused section of the coal bin. His wife and daughters prayed both day and night, either at church, where they managed to spend some hours during the day, or at home before the statue of St. Anthony that was kept on the bureau with a holy candle burning continually at its feet. Since the war, and mostly because of their mother's insistence, Anthony and Robert became more devout in their attendance at church. They went regularly every Sunday morning for communion. Bertocci had ceased to pray shortly after the war was into its fourth month; he was now silent about the possible end of the war and what God could do to help it come to an end, or to protect the lives of the men who fought in it. He became cynical even in his silence. He criticized his family's devotion, not with words, but subtly, by leaving the table when the mention of God found its way into conversation or by getting out of bed and leaving the room to sit in the parlor while his wife prayed before the statue. His cynicism caused him to eat less and he found fault with almost everything that he did eat. He went on with his life in an indifferent but pensive lassitude until finally, after having sat up one entire night in his armchair, the Zenith turned down low beside him, he asked Anthony the next morning to sit with him alone at breakfast before leaving for work. It was the first of October.

The decision to make wine, he told his son was made after he had grown convinced of the futility in hoping the war would end. In Europe and in the Pacific it would go on, he reasoned, for maybe five or six more years, and whatever reason one gave to its carnage it would cause more and more death. Roberto, too, would be called to serve in it. In the end—which he would probably not see nor cared whether he did see—nothing would be gained. There was no reason to pray for peace as they did every day, he went on, for God was as absurd as the carnage he was asked to end. Anthony listened to this as if he had heard it too many times and, when his father finished talking, he got up out of his chair to leave.

"You stay," said the father loudly. Anthony said nothing. He was sullen, and he sat back uneasily in his chair. His fingers played with the edge of the plate in front of him.

"You will be of age when the month is done," the father went on. "Because of this, I will sign the papers for you to join the navy."

Anthony looked across at him. His father's face was grave in the morning light lacing in through the curtains of the kitchen window. His eyes were watery and the lids were heavy and, when he spoke, the stubble of gray beard moved like a shadow upon his chin.

"Do you want me to do this, Antonio?" he asked solemnly.

Anthony looked up from his plate. "I should have gone with the others," he said.

The father leaned back in his chair.

"You will wait for the army?" he asked.

Anthony started to speak. He stopped, then he said, "No, I want the navy before I'm taken."

The father leaned forward again.

"Before you will go then," he said calmly, "I have decided to make *vino*. For you." He placed his hands on top of the table. "Only," he continued, "if you will help me."

The son was quiet. Finally, confused, he said, "I don't understand."

"It is all right that you do not understand," the father said.

Anthony was silent again. After a while he got up out of his chair, walked around the table and stood above his father. "All right," he said. He looked away for a moment, then he added, "Yes, I will help you. Because you cannot do it alone."

vi

Bertocci decided to use his own savings to buy the grapes. His wife argued against it, saying the money could be used to make repairs on the house. Bertocci refused to listen to her and went on to figure the amount of wine he would try to make on the basis of what money he had to spend. With pencil and paper and with Anthony's help he came to the point where he could choose one of two kinds of grapes. The muscats he knew would yield as much juice as the zinfandels, but the zinfandels would produce a drier wine, one with which he was familiar, since he had twice before made the same kind in Naples with his father. It took only minutes then to decide against the muscats. Next, he calculated what the probable yield would be from a twenty-six-pound bushel, and found he could get almost two gallons of juice if the grapes were good. Because of the war, he knew the dealers would charge what they could, since the shipment from California would probably be the last. Still, they could not ask for more than three dollars a bushel, even for the high-quality zinfandels. The barrels would cost five dollars each, not much more, and after he hired the crusher he would have a few dollars left over.

The wine press, Bertocci decided, could be borrowed from his fourth cousin. They had never been on friendly terms, and their only mutual concern, which brought them together for a short time after war with Italy had been declared, was the plight of their common relatives living in Naples. Their correspondence had lasted only a few days. It took place through the efforts of Anthony, who carried their terse and casual messages from one household to the other until finally, because both agreed they could do nothing for the relatives, they had nothing more to say.

Anthony had been told now to ask the cousin for the use of the press. The loan was refused. Bertocci asked again to borrow the press, but this time he promised to give the cousin two gallons of wine for its use. The cousin agreed, and Robert and Anthony, in a Ford sedan borrowed from a neighbor, drove across town, disassembled the press and returned it to their home, where Bertocci reassembled it in the cellar. The neighbor had been eager to loan the automobile after he, too, was promised two gallons of wine. He said nothing about the gasoline the boys had used, but Bertocci offered to pay for the gas when he asked again if the automobile could be borrowed on the fifteenth of October, the day the grapes were to arrive from California. The neighbor, who was not certain if he needed his car on that particular day, said he would consider the loan when the time came. Despite this uncertainty, Bertocci, laughing inwardly to himself, felt he could easily persuade the neighbor to give up his automobile for two more gallons of wine. He would see.

After he had figured what the total cost of making the wine would be, he sat with his wife and explained to her, dollar by dollar, how the money would be spent. They were alone in the house, and Bertocci spoke with enthusiasm of the details of his investment. When he was through talking there was a long silence, and finally an argument followed. His wife insisted again they should not spend money on wine. Instead, she said, it should be used to fix the house. Winter was coming on and the old clapboards needed repair. The brick chimney needed straightening too, and the little bathroom outside the kitchen in the back hall, where it was miserably cold in the winter, could use a small oil stove to keep it warm—at least during the time while someone was bathing in the tub. She went on to say that the amount of wood Anthony and Robert had sawed from a section of an old pinewood telephone pole was not enough kindling to take them through the winter. More coal for the furnace would be needed as well. To all this Bertocci said nothing.

When his wife had finished, he told her he wanted to make the wine now while their son was still at home, for after he was gone they would at least have a wine in whose body would be present part of his labor. Hearing this, the wife lifted herself from the chair, screaming that he was a fool. Bertocci threw back his head, bit his knuckles and shook them to heaven. He swore to the world in Italian that it had gone mad and that his wife had gone mad with it. Then he yelled that she was the fool, and that she prayed to a God who cheated them. He said in Italian, with a force that made his face redden: "You cannot see the absurdity in the war! You cannot see the arrogance of men on both sides who have caused it! You cannot see how the feeling of patriotism is used as a tool upon the lives of everyone, and upon the lives of all soldiers, and so because of it, a soldier's death is more absurd. Pray for peace," he yelled. "And you are fools." He pounded the top of the table with his fist until it shook through its legs to the floor. "I will make wine," he yelled. "It is my right and it will have in it the blood of my son!"

There had been little said about the wine at supper that night. It was mentioned only that Anthony would have to drive the father to the freight yards to buy the grapes.

Early the next Friday morning, after Anthony had called the arsenal and told his foreman that he was sick and would not be in to work until the following Monday, he went to the neighbor and promised, as the father told him to, two more gallons of wine for the use of the sedan. The loan was made without hesitation and the three of them— the father, Anthony and Robert, who was kept out of school to help—got into the borrowed automobile, turned up the street and left the neighborhood. They reached the big iron gate of the freight yard some time after the first boxcars had already been opened. Bertocci, who wanted to arrive before the seals on the freight-car doors were broken, sat impatiently in the front seat of the sedan, looking out the window. He sensed the excitement and asked quickly that Anthony park as soon as he could find room.

Anthony made the turn and drove carefully through the gate into the complex of tarpaulin-covered vans, automobiles, and open-rack pickup trucks. Some of the trucks were backing to the open doors of the freight cars, while others, having been loaded, pulled out into the yard and grinded away. Here and there a street peddler, his push-cart loaded with its five or six bushels of table grapes, avoided the maneuvers of the horse-drawn teams working into position against the freights. Small groups of men, most of them Italians wearing baggy, black cotton trousers and brown felt hats, were standing out of the traffic near the freights talking about the qualities of the wine they hoped to produce and the subtle virtues of the grapes they intended to buy to produce it. Those who had bought their grapes were in the process of carting them away. Fathers and sons, entire families—even strangers who had gone into partnership to divide the labor—were loading the sedans, lifting the bushels into the trunks and into the rears of the cars where the seats had been removed, and onto the flat boards of the trucks and the wagons. A few men stood in the open doors of the freights beside their grapes, waiting for a wagon or truck to ease in, ready to load up and return to their homes.

But the buying and selling continued and there was argument everywhere: inside the freight cars, alongside the empty tracks where clusters of men waited for the arrival of the last cars, and among the automobiles and trucks that were parked throughout the yard. The Italians argued among themselves as fiercely as with the dealers, but among the dealers the consciousness for money on both sides sharpened thought and triggered acute tempers. Heads shook in response to excessive prices, and hands gestured continually. There were times when the eyes of some men widened in the excitement of a bargain won, or narrowed miserably after the brief possibility of a victory was lost to the stubbornness of a determined dealer. From inside the freight cars came the sound of men swearing to heaven, to God, and to the saints of Italy and of the world; there was also the laughter of other men who, having found the tool of their dealers' weakness, had used it effectively and so had won their bargains easily.

But everyone was keyed to the same purpose, the atmosphere of which rose out of the fruity smell of harvest that had given its yield some three thousand miles away. It rose out of the jostling motion of the trucks and the automobiles, and out of the grinding steel rims of the wagons turning on the cobbles. It resounded in the sudden backfire of an old Ford gone off unnoticed in the windless air, and in the clanking of a boxcar door, lumbering open for the first time since it had been slammed shut in the freight yards of California. It was in the ripping of dry wood when a bushel was snapped open with a crowbar for the first time since it had been nailed closed in some

vineyard valley of San Joaquin or on the slopes of Mendo-
cino. It was in the wood of the boxes, and in the paper-
stenciled faces of the vineyard girls who stood eternal
among the rows of blue zinfandels; and last, it was in the
garagelike enclosure of the freight cars rife with the evi-
dence of the earth, the grapes themselves.

Anthony pulled into a space between two loaded wagons and parked. Slowly, the father opened the door of
the automobile and got out.

"I will do the buying. You will listen and say nothing,"
he said. The boys replied that they would not interfere,
and got out. The three of them made their way alongside
the wagons and turned out into the yard and into the
milling groups of men. Bertocci stopped now and then to
talk with the men. He asked about prices and about the
condition of the shipments that had already come in. Finally he saw a freight car from which a loaded truck was
pulling away. It was the freight closest to them, and Bertocci, thinking the truck was probably not the first to have
loaded there, thought his chances would be better in bar-
gaining for what grapes the dealer might have left on his
hands.

"We will begin with this one," he said. He reached for
the ladder laying up to the open door and, with the two
boys following, made his way up into the freight car.
When he got to the edge of the door, the dealer, who was
waiting, reached down and took him under the arms.

"*Buon giorno*," the dealer said loudly, condescendingly.

Bertocci straightened up in front of him and, looking
suspiciously into his red face, knew he was not an Italian.

"*Coma sta, pisan*," the dealer said. "*Co-ma-sta*," he
laughed, and led Bertocci further into the boxcar. "You
have come in time, *pisan*. I have only a few left. *Co-ma-
va*," he added abruptly.

Bertocci pulled his arm away. "I am well," he said.

"You are impatient, my friend," the dealer said. He broke into false laughter, and his red, purple-veined face bore down on Bertocci, who stood much shorter only inches away. "Your sons?" he asked, turning to the boys.

"They are my sons," the father said.

"They will help make the *vino* with you, huh?"

"Yes," the father said calmly. "We will make two barrels."

"How many gallons?"

"There will be fifty gallons in each barrel."

"You will need about fifty-five bushels."

"We will need forty-eight bushels for this, if the grape is good," Bertocci said.

"Well, I have what you need, *pisan*," the dealer said, laughing. "You will make a good dago red from my grapes."

Bertocci became uneasy now. "You will not call it dago red, *Signor*," he said calmly.

The dealer, still smiling, looked to the rear of the freight car. "It is all wine, my friend. Wine. I mean nothing by it," he said. "Here, look what I have for you." He pointed to the remaining boxes stacked against the wall. "They're big zinfandels with plenty of juice."

The father could see there were at least fifty or sixty bushels and knew he could probably get the lot at a good price. Disregarding his growing dislike for the dealer, he decided to sample his grapes. He walked to an open box on top of a stack. The boys and the dealer followed. "I will taste," he said. The dealer picked out a bunch of grapes, put one into his mouth and began to suck loudly, as Bertocci looked at him with disgust.

"Sweet, my friend," the dealer said, smacking his lips. He chewed rapidly into the husk, sucking all the while. Then pushing the husk with his tongue out onto his lips, he took it between his fingers and threw it to the floor, spitting out a spray of gritted seeds that landed on Bertocci's cuff. "I am sorry, my friend. The seeds are sour," the dealer said. "Here, let me help you a little." He took hold of Bertocci's cuff and began to rub it with his palm. "But the seeds will not affect the juice, *pisan,*" he said.

"It is all right," the father said. "Please, I will taste your grapes now." He reached into the box, and lifting out a bunch of grapes, raised it to his nose and breathed in the aroma of the husk. He then carefully removed one from the bunch, and between his forefinger and thumb squeezed it slowly until the husk split and the yellow pulp eased itself out onto his palm. He looked at the pulp and rolled it gently across his palm. The boys moved in close to him and watched silently. He put the pulp into his mouth and his lips began to work as it broke apart, filling his mouth with its juice and the sour taste of the crushed seeds. Finally he swallowed. He put the husk into his mouth and chewed again. The husk was tough, he thought, and it was sour too, but since it would contribute little to the overall character of the wine, he did not worry about this. The sweetness of the pulp was almost what he desired, but he was not concerned about this either. He was concerned mostly with the amount of water released from the pulp, and he thought it was too much. He swallowed the remaining husk, and looking at the bunch of grapes which he held up in front of him again, he decided there was no need in tasting another. "I will not buy," Bertocci said.

"Wait, *pisan.* I have others," the dealer said, taking him by the arm.

"I will not buy!"

"You taste the others, here." The dealer started to open another box.

"It is no use. They are all from same region," Bertocci said.

"They're from California, my friend. There is no difference in regions." The dealer looked confused. "Look," he said, "I'll give you a good buy. Besides, there's a war on and it'll be the last shipment. You should buy now."

"These are San Joaquin grapes," Bertocci said.

"So they are," the dealer said, tearing at the box cover with his crowbar.

"I will buy grapes only from the hillside," Bertocci said.

"There's no difference, I tell you. They're the same. They'll give you the same wine."

"San Joaquin will give you water," Bertocci said. "The land is flat there."

"You're buying zinfandel, my friend. What do you want for this kind of money, *romanee*?"

"I know nothing of *romanee*. I will buy only grapes with little water, not from San Joaquin."

"These grapes will give you a good dago red. Believe me, you will be pleased."

"You will not call it dago red."

"Whatever you like, but if you buy you will be pleased."

"I will not be pleased," Bertocci said, turning towards the door. "With you or your grapes."

The dealer took him by the arm again. "Listen, mister," he said, "I don't mean to hurt your feelings. Here's what I'll do. I'll give you five bushels extra . . . no, wait a minute. I'll give the whole lot to you. All I have left." He wiped his forehead. "You wanted forty-eight bushels, right? That comes to . . . let me see . . . ninety-six bucks. Well, I'll throw in the extra ten bushels for a buck apiece. What'ya say? Actually you're gitting five bushels for nothing. I'm giving 'em to you. Good deal, huh? Take them off my hands. What'ya say, the whole lot for one hundred and six bucks."

Bertocci straightened the front of his coat. "I do not want San Joaquin grapes. They are useless."

The dealer threw his hands to his head. "You guineas are all alike," he said.

"And you, my friend," Bertocci said, "are a fool." He placed the bunch of grapes back into the box. "Come," he said to his sons, "we will try the others."

It was mid-afternoon before Bertocci found a dealer who had the grapes he desired. They were probably grown on the slopes around Sonoma or in the Livermore region, he thought. He was not sure, but he had tasted conscientiously from about ten separate bushels and when he was convinced of the possibilities in the sample grapes, he completed his tasting. He was satisfied. He had found all of the grapes equally good. The density of the must and sugar of all he had tasted was balanced delicately, and the husks were less sour than those he had been sampling all morning. They were drier grapes, though, drier than what he was looking for, and he knew he would need more than he had figured on, since the yield per bushel would be less than the yield from the wetter grapes. But the price was good and when he considered the quality of new wine they might produce, he decided to buy ten bushels over his initial estimate to make up for the difference in yield.

At first there was some disagreement in price when Bertocci said he would need more grapes than those he had planned on buying. He had found prices in the yard ranging between two and two-and-a-half dollars for a twenty-six-pound bushel. He knew he could not pay two-and-a-half and then hire a wagon for another fifteen dollars to carry the grapes home; but he bargained successfully and finally the dealer agreed to sell at two dollars and a quarter providing Bertocci rent his wagon and driver and load the wagon himself. Bertocci agreed. He slowly counted off the bills out of his purse, paid the dealer, and took his receipt. The dealer put out his hand. "You have fine zinfandels there. I hope your wine is good."

"*Grazie,*" Bertocci said. He shook the dealer's hand. "We will try."

The father rode in the wagon with the Negro while the boys followed behind in the automobile. There had been little traffic on the back streets they had chosen as a route home, and although it was late afternoon, they arrived in the neighborhood while the sun was still shining and the air was unseasonably hot. Since they had no tarpaulin with which to cover them, the father worried about the condition of the grapes exposed to the sun. There were a dozen or more boxes that were open, and if the grapes in these were damaged by the sun, Bertocci knew the wine, too, could be affected even though they would yield only a part of the total juice. In his concern, he had asked the Negro to drive the horse a little faster lest the exposed grapes shrivel before they could be stored in the shade of the elm, where he planned to stack them for the night.

The Negro did as he was asked. Periodically he had brought the mare to a gallop and had kept her there until he could see the sweat working out from under the collar and wetting the black leather straps of the halters. When he saw this, he would ease her into a walk until her strength came back, then he would gallop her again. This intermittent galloping and walking was maintained for well over a half hour. The father had remained silent, speaking only to give directions, but when they had reached the outskirts of the neighborhood and he was satisfied that his grapes would not be damaged, he took the Negro by the arm and thanked him openly.

It was a few hours before dusk when they turned into the sloping street. They moved past the figures of neighborhood men in shirtsleeves standing along the curbs and behind the picket fences of the small front yards, and past the old red brick tenement house on the corner, where bare-armed women leaned on the sills of the open windows. Some of the men in the yards were burning leaves, but when they saw the wagon rattling by and Bertocci sitting up in the seat beside the Negro, they ceased their work and leaned silently on the handles of their rakes as if they leaned on the tops of shepherd's crooks, watching. A few of them knew Bertocci and had somehow heard the news that he was going to make wine, but having passed it off as rumor, they had forgotten about him. Now, with the wagon lumbering by loaded to the racks with the bright pinewood boxes of zinfandels glaring in the sunlight, they took notice in their surprise that the rumor had proven true. As for the women who spoke to each other in a clatter across the sills, some laughed in their disbelief that the wine would ever be made. Below in the street, children ran alongside of the wagon, jeering at the Negro, who began to swear as he reined in the mare against the sudden descent of the load when they made the turn, and against the rage of a chow dog that barked savagely at the clopping hooves of the tired horse. The car followed closely behind the wagon, and slowly, the procession made its way down the noisy street. When they finally reached the bottom of the hill the father motioned to the Negro, pointing to the yard where they would unload the grapes. The Negro nodded, pulled back lightly on the reins and guided the horse and wagon up to the open gate. They were home.

vii

The odor of grapes rose sweetly above the stacks of pinewood boxes, mingled with the scent of the elm and the leaves and the livid grape pulp which had burst under foot and lay scattered and bleeding in the grass. There was the sweat of the boys and their father and of the Negro too, pungent against the languid composite of odors that hung like a scented shroud about the small yard where the boxes were being stacked. All three of them wore T-shirts. They had unloaded the wagon without interruption, passing the bushel pinewood boxes from hand to hand—the father stacking the boxes under the elm in the shade, the oldest and the tallest of the two boys receiving the bushels of grapes from the Negro who stood on the tailboard of the wagon, and the next son working in between the father and the tallest son—and all three of them silent save for their breathing, which rose and fell with the hefting of the boxes as they were passed into the open arms of the next man. The T-shirts were sweated through and were splotched purple by the grapes which had crushed against them. In the mid-October heat and in the thin curtain of dust rising from beneath their shuffling feet from the stubbled dry earth of the yard, in the atmosphere of completion when the last box had been unloaded, they moved out of the twilight and sat beneath the elm among the rows of boxes, the father choosing to stand, looking at his investment with a critical, brooding concern.

Domenick Sardo had watched the unloading with envy. He stood behind the fence half hidden by the tree, counting the bushels as they were handed down from the wagon. He calculated that there were at least fifty boxes of grapes, but since he knew nothing about their quality, he could not figure the possible amount of wine each bushel would yield, and he became disconcerted. He had an idea of what they might have cost Bertocci, and he knew, because of the war, that the recent shipment from California would probably be the last. The dealers, he thought, realizing this, must have gotten a high price even for the poorer quality grapes. In his uncertainty, and because of his jealous anger, he wished miserably that Bertocci had been forced to buy the inferior grapes so that the wine he would labor to produce would in the end become worthless, a bad wine.

He became agitated. He wanted to know for certain if the grapes were inferior, and in his desire to taste one he thought of reaching over the fence and taking a bunch from one of the open boxes nearby. Finally, surreptitiously, his arm reached out from behind the tree. When Bertocci turned to place another box on the stack, Sardo withdrew his hand. He tried a few more times, but when he failed to steal a bunch in this way, he decided to wait until they finished unloading, or for nightfall when it would be possible to steal even a bushel.

During the hour and a half it had taken to unload the wagon the shoemaker had said nothing, neither to the boys nor to the father who worked only a few feet away from him on the other side of the fence. Bertocci had seen the Sicilian standing behind the tree, with his small frame partly hidden and his head looking out cunningly from time to time. He had given the shoemaker no notice except to let him know by one prolonged stare when he had first seen him that he knew he was there and cared nothing for his presence. When the last box had been unloaded and they were resting, the father turned to look at Sardo, who had stepped completely out from behind the tree. He was smiling. In the reddening dusk his dark face reflected the texture of oiled leather. He wore his shaggy cap pulled down almost to his eyebrows, and his hands played nervously round the tops of the pickets as he looked over the fence into the sweating face of Bertocci.

"*Granello d'uva*, Ciro," he said excitedly. "Zinfandel, yes?"

Bertocci looked away. "*Si*, zinfandel," he said tiredly.

"They have big size, Ciro. *Sono pieni di succo.* No?"

Bertocci turned to look at the Sicilian, who had reached across the fence and was passing his fingers over the grapes in one of the open boxes. "They will give what juice is in them to give," he answered. "I do not know what that will be."

"They are firm, Ciro."

"They are what they are," Bertocci said in Italian.

"Sweet—no, Ciro?" the shoemaker asked rapidly. "Much dry, yes? Good *vino* from these, no, Ciro?"

"They will give what they will give."

"But you have tasted, Ciro. Before you buy, no?"

"I have tasted many zinfandels today, Domenick Sardo," Bertocci said exhaustively. He watched the shoemaker's hand feel among the bunches, lift under them and squeeze and tap them lightly with his fingers.

"You will not touch the zinfandels, Domenick Sardo," Bertocci said.

"I only feel, Ciro. *Bellezza! Una bellezza!*"

"You will not feel."

"*Bellissimo*, Ciro." The shoemaker withdrew his hand from the box and gestured with his opened palm. "Maybe I taste then. Yes?"

"*Vai! Vai!*" Bertocci yelled.

The shoemaker smiled. "Ciro," he said, "I am happy if you want that I help with your vino. I only want to taste *d'uva* now."

Bertocci clenched his fists. "You will not taste, Domenick Sardo! *Vai! Vai!*" he yelled.

The shoemaker threw both arms out, his hands open. Then, pulling back his head with his eyes closed and his thin voice rising to exaggeration, he yelled, "*Buoni grappoli d'uva*, Ciro!" When he finished saying this he dropped one hand into the box and grabbed for a bunch of grapes. Bertocci, exasperated, lunged forward, his fingers spread for the shoemaker's throat. Sardo pulled his arm back across the fence, and with the bunch of grapes hanging from his fist, he sneered into Bertocci's face, turned, and ran into his house.

"*Sput'io te lo sangue!*" Bertocci yelled. "I spit in your blood!"

He ran out from under the elm swearing and came up to the Negro, who was standing beside the wagon. "I will put them in the cellar," he said. "You will help, yes?" He was breathing heavily.

The Negro agreed to help, although it was not part of the bargain, and when he said yes, Bertocci promised to pay him for the extra work. "We will begin now, then," the father said, both to the Negro and to his sons. The boys got to their feet. The father went into the house to open the cellar door. When he got it open, he found Anthony standing outside with a box of grapes in his arms, waiting to carry them in.

"Maybe I should take them down," Anthony said.

The father stood in the shadows of the cellar looking up the stairs into his son's face. "I will be all right," he said, breathing heavily.

"But it'd be easier if I took them down," Anthony said. He looked into his father's face. It was still sweating in the shadowy light of the cellar. The eyes were languid and heavy-lidded. They seemed as if they were about to close. Bertocci took out his handkerchief and drew it across his brow and across the back of his neck. He coughed once and then slowly wiped his mouth. "We will begin now," he said, folding the handkerchief and putting it back into his pocket. "You will take them down to me."

Anthony, who had been holding the bushel under his arms, made his way down the few wooden steps into the cellar.

"They will be put here," the father said. He motioned with his hand and Anthony walked across the earthen floor to the far wall, against which he set down the first bushel of zinfandels. "It is good," the father said. "There is plenty of room here for all of them."

The distance from the tree to the cellar was shorter than the distance had been from the wagon at the curb to the tree, so it took them only about one hour to carry all the boxes into the cellar, stack them against the wall and then pick up the grapes which had fallen onto the ground. The sun was down when they finished and the air was beginning to cool. A breeze wafted from the field in back of the houses carrying with it the scent of dry grass and the pungent odor of smoke that had lifted from the small fires of burning leaves smoldering now throughout the neighborhood. In the elm, a mass of leaves loosened free from their branches and floated down into the yard below. Anthony came out of the cellar and walked to the wagon. After a time the father too came out and walked quietly across the yard and stood under the elm alone. He rested against the tree, his head turned up toward the branches, and breathed in the leafy odor of dusk and October and the lingering trace of the zinfandels. The vinous aroma still rose from the clods of grass and from the porous stubble of sod near the cellar door where some of the grapes had been crushed by their feet and whose purple blood stained here and there the pebbly earth of the yard.

"We have done good," he said to the boys, who were standing by the wagon talking to the Negro.

"You'll have a good rest tonight," Anthony said.

"I will rest," the father said, coming up to them. "Now, my friend"—he gave his hand to the Negro—"I will pay you again."

"Yes suh," the Negro replied, taking his hand.

"You want how much?" Bertocci asked.

"Well, suh, maybe a dolla'." He paused, then he asked, "Too much, suh?"

"It is good," Bertocci said. "It is a good price for what you have done." He reached into his pocket and took out a crumpled bill, which he unfolded carefully. He looked at it deliberately and gave it to the Negro. "You are the lucky man," he said, laughing. "It is all that is left."

"Thank you, suh," the Negro said. "Much obliged." He climbed into the wagon seat, slapped the reins twice and the horse started to pull away from the curb.

"Wait," Bertocci called. He was opening his leather purse. "For you," he yelled. He took out the two remaining quarters and the one dime. Walking up to the wagon he handed the change to the Negro. "Take it. It is yours."

The Negro reached down and took the money. "Thank you, suh. I hope yuh'll make some good vinosuh." He slapped the reins again and the horse pulled away.

"*Buona sera*," Bertocci called after him, raising his hand. "We will make some good vinosuh. Yes!"

viii

It was near to half-past seven in the morning when the father and his two sons got out of bed, dressed, and after breakfast, went down into the cellar. Through a small window located in the foundation wall just above a stack of opened bushels, a beam of sunlight filtered down onto the exposed grapes. In the glare of this early light, penetrating feebly as it did through the motes of dust floating about the cellar, the grapes took on the color of artificial table fruit: a waxy, unreal blue against the white pine texture of the wooden boxes. When Bertocci saw them he began to feel excitedly among the bunches, wondering what had happened to his grapes during only one night in the cool of the cellar. He tasted from one bunch, then from another. He lifted the top box off the stack and tasted grapes from the box that had been under it. Their quality, he found, was the same as it had been in the freight car the day before. He looked up at the window and held his hand against the light. Now when he looked down at the shaded grapes, he was convinced that their strange color was caused by the light coming in through the cellar window. He was relieved. Still, while he adjusted the crusher, he asked Robert to cover with sheets of old newspapers all of the exposed grapes in the open boxes.

Opposite the boxes, under a single bare bulb whose cord hung from a nail that Anthony had driven into the overhead beam, the crusher stood where it had been placed on the floor the night before. It had arrived completely assembled from the hardware store where Bertocci had rented it. It was carried into the cellar and was wiped clean just after the Negro was paid. Now Bertocci cleaned it again. It was a small hand-operated crusher with a red oak hopper. Inside of the hopper, at the bottom, were two spike-lined intermeshing rollers. The hand crank was made of cast iron and it had a wooden handle grip of white oak at right angles to its end. The name, MICHIGAN, was casted into the metal across the front. It was a new crusher Bertocci had rented for half a day. He hoped to complete the crushing before this time, since he had yet to pay for the four barrels, which at this point had not yet arrived. After he paid for the barrels he would have no money left to pay for overtime on the crusher if he had to use it longer than he had planned.

At one time the father had considered letting his daughters help with the crushing. He decided that they could remove the leaves and cut off the thick woody stems that were attached to the grapes. It would go quicker. But he later changed his mind when he realized why he was making the wine in the first place. It was Anthony, he reasoned, who would not be present when the wine was ready to be drunk. Because of this, he wanted a wine whose nature was the outcome of a labor in which Anthony and Anthony alone would share. His wife had argued against this by saying it was foolish, since they would all drink of the wine when it was ready. But Bertocci rebuffed her angrily, first with argument and then finally with silence. She said no more about it, asking only that Bertocci allow Robert to help, since he too might be taken if the war continued. To this the father agreed, but only after he had thought about it for a week.

The crusher was lifted into place over an old thirty-gallon barrel that had been used some time before to make pickled peppers. The insides had been scoured clean and could be used now to hold the crushed grapes until the new barrels came. The father took a rag and again carefully wiped the inside of the crusher. Anthony then poured in the first quantity of grapes that he and Robert had already picked clean of leaves and stems. The father put down the rag. He took Robert's hand and, after placing it on the oak handle of the crank, told him to turn. In a while there was the sound of cracking stems, husks and splitting seeds, as the grapes went through the rollers and plopped like mush into the hollow of the barrel.

Before the hopper became empty, Anthony would pour in another portion of grapes. In this way Robert was forced to turn the crank for nearly fifteen minutes without stopping. When the motion of his hand started to slow down and he looked tired, the father asked him to rest and took over the crusher himself.

At the end of twenty minutes of steady work they had managed to fill the barrel with the first substance of crushed grape. This *spezzata,* the father told them it was called, filled the cellar with its fruity scent. Bertocci took in a slow, deep breath, with his eyes closed and his head tipping back under the bulb. He smiled, opened his eyes, and asked Anthony to help him lift the crusher off the barrel. When they got it onto the floor the father looked into the barrel, reached in and cupped out a handful of the crushed fruit. He could see that the husks were intensely purple on the outside and almost the color of blood on the inside. And the seeds, too, like the split pulps, were tinted reddish purple, soaked as they now were in their own newly released pigment and juice. The father raised his hand to his face and smelled the *spezzata* carefully. Then, as the two boys watched silently, he sipped quietly from the mixture of cool juice that filled the hollow of his palm. He smiled again. It tasted sweet, he thought, sweeter than he had hoped; yet in the sweetness there was the subtle taste of husk, fruity and delicately sour, and this was what he desired. He was satisfied.

At this point the father knew that he could not make a prediction concerning what the final character of the wine would be. The first pressing, even a third pressing, could bring out the adverse qualities of the grapes and destroy the qualities he desired in the new wine. In his uncertainty, while he waited for the barrels, he thought of pressing a portion of *spezzata* now, so that the possible character of the wine would show itself in the taste and quality of the new juice.

"Why is it the other barrels are not here?" he said absently, still scooping up handfuls of crushed grapes. "We can not finish if they do not come." The father took his hand out of the barrel, wiped it, and looked at the bushels of uncrushed grapes. He figured the time it would take to crush them. It was close to what he had expected, but he could not continue crushing, since there were no barrels into which they could put the *spezzata*. He would either have to wait for the delivery of the barrels—in which case he would have to pay for overtime on the crusher—or press the *spezzata* he had already produced. Finally, when five or six minutes had gone by, during which time he paced between the barrel and the press, he decided to squeeze the *spezzata*. If the barrels arrived in the meantime, he could go back to crushing the remaining grapes. If he went into overtime, he would raise the money somehow. He asked Anthony to take the bulb and cord and hang it over the press. When the light bulb was in place, the father, showing some excitement in his anticipation of what the new juice might prove, rolled the barrel on its bottom rim until it was opposite the press.

"Roberto," he said, "*secchia*, bring." He pointed to the five-gallon galvanized washtub hanging from a wooden peg that had been driven into a crack in the foundation wall. Roberto got the tub and brought it to his father, who was shifting the barrel into place beside the press.

"Here. Put it here," Bertocci said. "I empty *succo*." He tipped the barrel slowly. "Antonio," he said, pointing now to a piece of screening, "you bring." Anthony brought him the screening and, while the father tipped the top of the barrel toward the bucket, Anthony, without having to be told, held the screen mesh over the mouth of the barrel. The grape juice spilled over the rim, as husks, stems and uncrushed pulp remained behind the screen. When the father saw that there was no more juice to be taken from the crushed grapes, he tipped the barrel upright again. "There is little *succo*, but it is clear *succo*," he said. There was about three gallons of juice in the tub. "Bring the cup, Roberto," he said. Roberto brought the cup and handed it to his father. "Taste," the father said. He held the cup out to Anthony, who took it hesitantly.

"You want me to taste?" Anthony asked.

"Yes," the father said.

Anthony dipped the cup into the juice and slowly brought it up to his lips. His father watched him intently. Roberto smiled curiously as Anthony swallowed from the cup. When it was empty he handed it to his father, whose face was flaccid, and whose eyes reflected clearly the diffused glare of the bulb. He smiled. "You like it?" he asked calmly.

Anthony turned to Roberto, then looked at his father. "I don't know," he said, frowning. "It tastes a little sour."

The father did not smile now. "It can not be too sweet," he said. "It is all right for what I get now. When I get *vino nuovo* it will be sweet. Maybe too sweet then. We will see."

The father adjusted the bulb, letting it hang lower in order to see better while they filled the basket of the press. Then the three of them, each in turn, reached into the barrel and took out handfuls of crushed grape which they put into the basket of the press. When the basket was full, Anthony, under his father's directions, tamped down the *spezzata* with a piece of wooden two-by-four. "When it is squeeze now it is not the best *succo*," the father said. "It is not *vino*." He placed a pail under the little tin spout nailed to the bottom of the basket. "But I will try for it now anyway," he said, and he began to turn the press wheel.

It required only minutes to squeeze the first quantity of crushed grape. Taking the cup again the father dipped into the juice and tasted it carefully, sipping slowly from the cup until it was empty. His sons watched curiously. He passed the cup to Anthony. "You taste it now," he said, smiling. "It is not *vino nuovo*. But it is good."

Anthony filled the cup and drank. "It's not as sour, like before," he said, handing the cup back to his father.

"It is good *succo* for now," the father said.

"It's redder," Anthony said.

"Because of *belleto*. Here, Roberto, you taste." The father handed the cup to his younger son.

Roberto dipped, raised the cup to his mouth and drank it empty.

"You like it?" the father asked.

"It's good," Robert said. "Yes."

"It is good *succo*," the father said, nodding his head.

"Will you squeeze the rest?" Anthony asked.

"There is no need. I think we will make some good *vino* from these zinfandels. We will wait now for the barrels to come."

When the barrels did arrive Bertocci at first argued with the truck driver, but when the man explained the reason for his delay—a flat tire in the middle of town—the barrels were taken in. After Bertocci examined them and saw they were the six-hooped, charred distiller barrels he had ordered, he started to pay the driver. When he found that he had only nineteen dollars, he asked the driver to wait while he went upstairs to borrow a dollar from his wife. She took the money out of her savings, which amounted to some four and a half dollars. She had argued fiercely against her husband's request. Why were two barrels not enough if he was going to make only two barrels of wine, she asked repeatedly. Bertocci tried to explain to her that four barrels were needed to hold all of the crushed grapes while they fermented. Each barrel would be filled to half. After the fermenting stopped, he said, they would get enough new wine to fill two barrels completely. She found this difficult to understand, insisting that he tell her what he would do with the empty barrels.

"I will eat them," he said stubbornly in Italian.

Bertocci, happy with his victory over his wife, paid the driver.

They worked two hours more before the remainder of the grapes were crushed. The four fifty-gallon barrels had been filled to half capacity, allowing enough space for the grapes to rise during fermentation. The thirty-gallon barrel was loaded to half also, taking the extra grapes that Bertocci had bought to make up for the low yield of the somewhat dry zinfandels. But he was satisfied with the work and the amount of crushed grapes it had produced. He figured on at least one hundred gallons of wine, maybe a little more if there were more than one squeezing, but whatever the amount, he was almost sure the wine would have a uniform quality. He had periodically tasted the juice during the crushing and found it to taste the same from almost every box. The differences he had found were slight, some grapes being a little more sour than others. Yet he was happy with the balance, and with the low acidity. Acidity, or *di tannino*, as he explained to Anthony, if too high, would cause the wine to taste sour— more like vinegar than wine. "It will be right to stop it before it is vinegar," he said to the boys. "It is what *vino* is. It is the juice of the grape that has tried to become vinegar and failed." He smiled. "I must make sure it will fail."

ix

The grapes would start fermenting in about ten days, the father had said, after which they would rise each day to the top of the barrels, forming what was called a hat. It would be necessary then for Anthony and Robert to push the hat down in each barrel every morning and at the end of every day. This chore they did willingly, stirring and pushing with the wooden paddles the father had made from one of the boxes. They would listen, as they were asked to do, for the first minute explosion of gas from within the mass of crushed grapes, signaling that fermentation had begun. Anthony had been the first to hear this. It was on the seventh day, three days before his father's prediction, and it sounded to him like a snap, as if a small twig had been suddenly split in half. He bent his head lower and turned one ear to the barrel. There was another little explosion, then several more in succession until finally, recurring more rapidly now, they merged into a composite sound of exploding bubbles bursting out of the surface of the juice. He lifted the covers from the other three barrels and found that from the juice in these too came the same sound and the same popping of bubbles.

When the father came into the cellar, he too listened. "It has begun," he said with excitement. "It will go on for another week, maybe a few days more. But it will come. It is coming good now." He placed the lids back on the barrels. "You must push down more each day, Antonio," he said. "The juice is starting to give."

"Yes," Anthony said. He paused and then asked, "What do you think of it?"

"It is early to say. I will give it four, maybe five more days, then I will taste."

"What if it does not turn into wine?"

The father was silent; then he said, "I will put in sugar to make it ferment. It will help." He became pensive and thought of the possibility of having to add sugar. "But I wish not to do that," he said. "It is not good *vino* when all does not come from the grape, when you must put things in from the outside." He looked quietly at the barrels lined against the wall. "When one must do that," he said, "he has bought bad grapes."

"But you tasted the juice when we crushed," Anthony said. "You said it was good juice then."

"I be maybe wrong then."

"When will you know if you bought bad grapes?"

"I will wait until it is pressed. Then I can know what it can be in a year maybe, even if I must put in the sugar now."

"There's no way of telling now what it's going to be?"

"No," the father said. He appeared agitated. "I can know only what it can be, not what it will be. And this I can not be sure of now."

Anthony adjusted one of the lids on the barrel. "I hope it's good wine," he said. "For you."

"I hope it is good *vino* for us both." The father was silent, then he said calmly and with finality, "I hope it is good *vino* for us all."

Although Anthony knew nothing about wine except what his father had told him—and this information was hardly enough in helping him to know what to look for in the taste of fermenting must—he sampled a taste from the barrels each day until the afternoon of the fifteenth day. It was a Saturday, and the juice had reached that point in its fermentation when it could be called wine. It had stung Anthony's throat upon his first swallow, but gradually, as he continued to sip from the tin cup, he became used to the sting, which before long he began to enjoy. He filled the cup again and offered it to Robert, who stood back watching.

"Here. Drink some," Anthony said. "It's good."

"A little," Robert said. He hesitated, sipped, then swallowed once, coughing spasmodically back into the cup. The wine shook out onto his face, trickled down his chin like a streak of blood and stained the front of his shirt. "It's . . . too . . . strong," he coughed, handing the cup back to Anthony.

"It's wine," Anthony said. Laughing, he raised the cup and he drank it empty.

In the following half hour he drank four more cups of the new wine before he experienced the dizziness. Suddenly a wave of nausea passed through him and he fell against the wall, reeled once, and dropped the cup of wine. He grabbed at his stomach, moaned and began to slip down against the wall. Robert reached out for him, then lurched back as a stream of vomit came belching out of his brother's mouth. Anthony reeled again, and in the strange weightlessness of his fall, he grabbed instinctively for the stanchion post nearby, missed, and spun into the thirty-gallon barrel that was directly in front of him.

His chest had hit square on against the rim of the barrel, causing it to tip over away from the wall. Robert ran out of the cellar when he saw this. When he returned with his father they found Anthony lying beside the overturned barrel, face down in the wet mass of husks and stems. There was a black stain on the cellar floor, where the spilt wine had soaked into the earth.

"*Ubriacone,*" the father yelled. He leaned over and got his hands under Anthony's arms. "Here, Roberto," he said, "help him pick up."

They managed to get Anthony to his feet and propped him against the wall. His eyes were closed and his head hung loosely to one side.

"*Ubriacone,*" the father said angrily. "You are drunk," and he began hitting his son on the face with his opened hand.

"Wake," he yelled. He hit Anthony's face again, this time with the back of his hand. Anthony opened his eyes weakly, drawing his head away from the sting of the hand.

"*Ubriacone cotta,*" the father yelled again. He released his hold on Anthony's shoulder and held him against the wall by the throat. "*Ubriacone,*" he said. "Wake." He hit him once more, rested, and then began hitting him again. "*Ubriaco cotta,*" he yelled finally. He stopped hitting and slowly opened one of Anthony's eyes with his fingers. "Wake, Antonio," he said tiredly. He was breathing heavily. His face was grave and it had gone flush, and in his eyes, which began to blink rapidly, there was a trace of water. "*Figlio*, Antonio," he said hoarsely. "You must wake up."

Anthony opened his eyes. He could feel the pain working into his nose. "You have drink too much, Antonio," the father said calmly. "Come, we will put you in your bed."

Anthony staggered from the wall and was led to the stairs. After stumbling against the walls of the stairway on their way up, and finally falling through the kitchen door onto the floor, he was picked up by Robert and his father and put into bed. When he woke the next morning with the bridge of his nose swollen painfully and the sour trace of lingering nausea still working in his belly, he could remember only drinking the first few cups of wine and the first dizzying sickness that had come over him. What happened after that he was unable to remember for certain, but he did remember—or had the vague feeling that he dreamed it—that someone had been hitting him on the face while he spun through the vertigo of his drunkenness. What he did know, or surmised for certain by the silence of his father at the breakfast table, was that he had caused his father's anger, and he wondered now if he had done anything for which he would be punished. While he ate his breakfast he tried not to look across the table, but time and again, the reason for which he was beginning to understand, he found himself glancing furtively over his plate at his father. He felt embarrassed and uncomfortable, not for what he had done or thought he had done, but for the impulse he could feel inside of him—to leave his chair, take his father by the throat and hit him as he now knew he had been hit himself.

Bertocci finished his bread, drank his last cup of black coffee and leaned back in his chair. He looked at each of his sons. The daughters were not present. They had not yet returned home from early mass. Robert sat between his mother and Anthony, his head lowered and his hands quietly folded in his lap. His mother looked at Anthony, whose eyes lowered slowly and stared at the uneaten food on the plate in front of him.

"*Mangia*," the mother said softly. "You must finish."

Anthony looked up, "I'm not hungry," he said.

"But you must eat, Antonio," the mother said.

He raised his voice a little. "I am not hungry. I don't want to eat," he said.

"When you come from the church, then. It will keep for you on the stove, Antonio."

"I won't be hungry then either," Anthony said harshly.

The father placed both hands on the edge of the table. "*Vino* is not to get drunk," he said suddenly, loudly, looking directly across at Anthony. "It is that for others. Not for us."

Anthony felt the inside of his throat tighten. He squeezed his fist under the table and with a deliberate motion of his head turned from his mother and looked into his father's eyes. He swallowed once, then he said calmly, "I didn't know it would happen." He stuttered a moment, then added, "I am sorry."

"You have ruined much wine," the father said.

Anthony lowered his head. "I am sorry for that," he said.

"You are sorry, but the wine is gone."

The father looked at his wife, then he turned to Anthony, took his hands off the table and leaned back. "I beat you for your own good, Antonio," he said.

"I don't remember that," Anthony said.

"It is good then," the father said. "Now," he got up out of the chair, "when you come from church we will begin the squeezing." He walked around to Anthony and placed his hand on his shoulder. "Only if you want to help, Antonio. I will wait until you come back."

Anthony looked at his mother. After a long silence, he got up and faced his father. "I will help you, as I said I would, only because you can not do it alone." He walked out of the kitchen, put on his coat and left for church.

X

When Anthony returned from mass he and Robert and their father went down into the cellar to begin the pressing of the fermented grapes. First they wracked off the new wine, which filled one barrel completely. They then emptied the substance from the three remaining barrels into two barrels in preparation for squeezing. This marc, or *la vinaccia,* as the father called it—composed of the fermented grapes, their husks and stems, the many seeds that did not get crushed, and the fermented flesh of the pulp—would be pressed to release the new wine held within it. When this was done, when all of the marc was squeezed, its yield would then be mixed with the new wine already wracked off. This mixing, the father explained, had to be done because the wine pressed from the *vinaccia* would have a strong taste of the husk, a taste different from that of the wracked-off wine. The mixing of the two would create a blend of the right flavor, or body.

The husky taste could not be avoided, the father said. It would come from the skins of the squeezed grapes and it was desired, but he said the more times one pressed the *vinaccia* the more this taste would dominate the wine released from it. Because of this, he was not sure he would bring it through for more than one squeezing. It would depend on what the quality of wine would be after the first pressing.

But he was not concerned with the amount of new wine he could press. He knew he could not get a full barrel because he had lost everything fermenting in the thirty-gallon barrel, but if he got enough wine from the first squeezing—at least three-fifths of a barrel, maybe a little more, as he now figured on getting, and it tasted right—he would be satisfied.

The father had tasted the wine faithfully every day following the moment when it first started to ferment. He had not had to add sugar and for this he was grateful. So far then, everything pointed to the possibility that he would get all that he wanted from the first pressing. Yet it would age and he knew that this could give him a wine for which he would have no desire. It could turn even to vinegar, he told his sons. But he was happy with its taste as it stood now. It was fruity and a little dry with a hefty almost sweetening aftersting of alcohol.

Anthony said little as he and Robert filled the basket of the press with the first quantity of dripping marc. When they finished, they stepped back curiously and allowed the father to get into position beside the press. He showed some excitement, which he tried to conceal by rolling up his sleeves carefully and then smiling blankly at the boys. He adjusted the bulb now by letting it hang lower over the press. Then he loosened his belt, spit into each of his palms and rubbed them together until he could feel the heat work through to the moisture on his skin.

"We will see now what we get from *la vinaccia*," he said, as though talking to himself. He reached up and took hold of the press wheel handle and the first surge of energy diffused into the muscles of his arm and traveled down into his knobby-haired fist of fingers and bone. He paused and wiped his forehead with his free hand, then, exerting himself to loosen the stiffness of the old press, the initial moment of the torque he produced imparted itself to the iron handle and the process began: the wheel

turning through several slow degrees of arc; the fist holding and turning at the end of the bare arm; the forward
heave of the shoulder behind the extension of arm and
fist, and the chest rising to the unity of force and purpose
—all slow rhythm and expectation.

The movement of the aged wood and cast-iron machin-
ery of the press was contiguous: the downward thrust of
the pressure cover, noiseless and supple at first but coming down inch by inch against the crushed grape and the
twiggy pulp, wet but not yet bleeding; and the sound
coming now like the unoiled links of a rusty chain. The
hand turned the press wheel as the greased threads of the
screw rod disappeared through the iron frame of the cross-
bar above the basket, the screw worming downward
against the pressure cover, and this against the grape beneath it, pressing to merge as one the ghost of former
wines interred in the grain of the wood, released now by
the anointment of new juice to bring forth the scent of
soaked wood. Then the odor of bleeding grapes began to
leave the interstices of the press, and in a short while the
first droplet of wine trickled down the tin spout nailed to
the bottom of the basket. It fell like a liquid jewel into
the galvanized pail where it came to rest clean and red
and perfectly alone against the glare of the metal upon
which it lay. The father looked at the droplet and then
continued to turn the press wheel, increasing his effort
against the handle. Gradually he could feel the grapes give
still further under the increased pressure as the cover
squeezed and pulverized the mass of blue husks, pulp,
seeds and stems into the complexity of new must. The
flow of the must began to increase too. It turned a darker
red now with its sudden concentration of pigment, flowing
like a ribbon of silk from the lip of the spout, seemingly
motionless in its descent from the spout, but then sizzling
like a streak of rain into the bubbling surface of new wine
rising steadily in the pail.

The father turned the press wheel until the marc was completely squeezed. When he saw what it had given— the pail was near to full—he realized he could get almost as much wine as he had estimated by bringing the *vinaccia* through only one squeezing. He looked into the barrels. "If *nuovo vino* from this is good," he said excitedly, "we can squeeze only once." He became enthused. He stooped down beside the pail and twirled his finger through the surface of the new wine. "We will see now what *la vinaccia* has given." He licked his fingers, looked up at his sons and smacked his lips. "I must have the cup, Antonio," he said, getting up. Anthony gave him the cup and he dipped it into the wine. He brought it up to his nose, sniffed it, and then lowered it to his lips. He sipped, smacked once and sipped again. Smiling, he drank a mouthful, which he sucked back and forth between his teeth, his cheeks puffing in and out rapidly. He swallowed, sipped again and smacked, as he nodded his head quickly. *"Perfecto,"* he said, "it is good." He drank the rest of the wine eagerly and handed the cup to Anthony. "You taste, Antonio," he said excitedly. Anthony remained silent, his hands down at his side. "Taste," the father said again.

Anthony became uneasy, shifting once on his feet and then putting his hands into his pockets. "My stomach doesn't feel good," he said.

"It will make you feel better if you take a little," the father said. "Here, drink." He held out the cup.

"I do not want to get drunk," Anthony said slowly.

"You will not get drunk, Antonio. Not like before. You drink now."

Anthony looked at Robert, who stood back in the shadows watching. "Let him taste it," he said stubbornly.

The father dipped the cup into the pail. "I want you to drink," he said emphatically, "not Roberto. Here!" He pushed the cup out in front of Anthony again. "It is your wine," he said forcefully.

Anthony looked down at the floor. "It is yours," he said. He was silent for a moment, then he said slowly, "It is what you have made for yourself."

The father reached out and took him by the shoulder. "I have made this for you," he said.

"I don't want to drink it," Anthony said.

"You will taste it, Antonio."

"I will get drunk again."

The father's eyes narrowed. "You will not get drunk," he said, raising his voice. "Here. You drink."

Anthony looked up at his father. "It is not for us to get drunk, you said."

The father was silent; a grave, saddened look came into his face. After a while he spoke, "I am sorry that I beat you, Antonio," he said.

Anthony turned away and there was another silence between them. The father put down the cup. "If you will not drink then we must finish here. Otherwise the *vinaccia* will sour," he said sternly. He looked at Robert. "You," he said, "you empty the basket. I will fill it." He turned to Anthony again. "You," he said loudly, "you will squeeze. Come."

They worked for the next four hours, the father taking over the press when Anthony got tired, and Robert filling and then emptying the basket after the marc had been thoroughly squeezed. They spoke little and worked nearly without interruption. Only once the mother came down into the cellar with a plate of cheese, cold meat and a loaf of bread. They rested and ate the food and then went back to work until all of the marc had been pressed. The total yield filled the fifty-gallon barrel to about four-fifths, exactly what the father had hoped. Now all that had to be done was to mix the wines together, and this the father did easily. The sons, meanwhile, filled about a dozen bushel boxes with pressed marc and dragged the boxes across the floor to the cellar door, where they were then carried up one by one and dumped in a corner of the yard. By the time they finished, the two barrels of wine were sealed and had been rolled into the little wooden enclosure of the coal bin.

The brothers came in from the yard and found their father standing pensively in the doorway of the bin. "This will be the wine cellar," he said. He motioned with his arms. "I will build the door here." His face was pale and his shoulders slouched downward. He unrolled his sleeves slowly, drawing first one and then the other down to his wrists. The sweat on his face began to cool. He took out his handkerchief and wiped his forehead carefully. He drew the handkerchief across his mouth, coughing deeply, folded it, put it back into his pocket and closed his eyes. He remained silent for some time before Anthony, who stood quietly watching him, decided to speak.

"Are you all right?" he asked.

The father opened his eyes, blinked as if coming out of a dream, and looked at his son. After a moment he spoke. "Sometimes, we do things that we do not mean to do." He turned and walked away slowly. When he got to the bottom of the stairs he stopped. He did not turn around, but stared up into the shadows of the stairway. "I am to be sorry, Antonio, that I beat you. And I think maybe we have worked for some good zinfandel." He coughed again, this time it was heavier, and made his way up into the house.

xi

Crouching behind a lilac bush that grew alongside Bertocci's house, Domenick Sardo had watched the pressing of the grapes through the cellar window. In his envy of Bertocci's having succeeded this far in his wine-making venture, the shoemaker felt an increasing need for vengeance. But it must take a form, he decided, that would not show the reasons behind it, for only in this way could he delude his neighbor into becoming a fool against his will.

Sardo thought about this for more than a week until one day, while he sat before his last repairing a shoe, he slipped into a deep reminiscence. He dreamily remembered a time in Italy, when he was a boy, when a traveling group of four Catholic priests, collecting alms during the Christmas season, were given overnight shelter in his house. His father, Belletino Sardo, a thin little man who moved about his small farm with an anxious determination, gained most of his income by processing limestones taken from the nearby fields, which were then baked, pulverized and put up into burlap bags for sale. Although he was not a rich man, he was able to provide for his family and at the same time maintain his self-sufficiency. There were always three or four goats about, a cow or two for milk and cheese, as many as fifty or sixty chickens and a warren housing no less than ten or fifteen domesticated rabbits. Occasionally, depending on the money needs of the family, Belletino would take his excess livestock to market. He was a serious worker who gave nothing away and asked for nothing. And his belief that "one should eat only if one worked" was as stringent a belief as was his determination never to deviate from it. In time, the parsimony of Belletino Sardo became legend throughout the countryside. It was said that he would rather let a man starve and die in his dignity than let him eat and live by the labor of another. In spite of his religious commitments, which consisted of half-hearted prayers and a few thousand lire grudgingly donated each year to the little Catholic church that served the area, Belletino's belief in

God was an otherwise abstract feeling that varied from deep aggravation to a helpless surrender when things on his land did not go as he would have liked. His view toward the clergy always was a practical one: priests, like himself, he reasoned, were men, and like all men they must eat to live. If there was no visible work they could show in providing for themselves, then they should go without until God—if there was one—decided their fate. On this particular night then, when the four traveling priests came to the house of Belletino Sardo, he provided for them in the best way that his beliefs would let him. He fed and watered the two mules that had drawn their cart. He had water heated so that they might cleanse themselves of the dust of the journey. He provided a room for them. He had a fire set in the stone hearth and fresh bedclothes put out for their use. When time came to sit and eat, he had his wife and daughters prepare a meal that was consumed hungrily.

When Domenick Sardo thought about all of this, he remembered that his father had at first shown a stubborn refusal to slaughter any animals to feed the priests. Meat, he reasoned, was a food that required much care and labor to produce. To give it away, especially to those who lived on the alms and labors of others, would be an act committed against his will. In compromise with his belief that one eats only when one works, he called Domenick aside and told him what he should do. In a small wooden hut where feed grains were kept lived several cats who fed on the rats and mice that at times raided the grains. Following his father's instructions, Domenick went out to the hut, slaughtered, skinned, and quartered four of the cats and presented them to his mother, as he was told, as the meat of four rabbits. The supper meal that Belletino Sardo had put out for the four priests then, consisted of homemade wine and bread, the meat of the four cats—

disguised unknowingly by his wife as rabbit—stewed in tomatoes, mushrooms and green peppers preserved from the family garden. Sardo remembered now that the four priests had shown no suspicion or distaste for the meal. As it was, surfeited by his father's generosity, they had not asked for alms. Instead, after the meal, they went to the room provided for them and slept. In the morning, refreshed by their sleep and filled with gratitude, they had kneeled before the house of Belletino Sardo and offered their prayers.

Sardo had the feeling now that somewhere hidden in this memory was the key to his vengeance against Bertocci. As he stared through the plate glass window to the street, his hammer poised above the shoe on his last, it came to him suddenly: "I will make him a gift!" he said in Italian, slamming the hammer on the sole of the shoe. "Si, a gift I will give him and it will honor the virtue of his wine!" He broke into hysteric laughter, closed his shop and went home.

Like most of the families in the neighborhood, the Bertoccis had had several pets over the years. The last was a mongrel dog that had in its later years developed a progressive form of arthritic lameness that eventually crippled the animal almost totally. It was able only to drag itself across the floor on its hind legs. This caused an irritable uneasiness in the household. Despite this, Bertocci, who had formed a deep attachment to the animal, held to the hope that it might some day be cured; but after several attempts by the veterinarian to alleviate the dog's suffering, it was decided that the disease had gone too far and the animal was sent off to be put away.

Bertocci, in his grief, went into a kind of restless mourning. His children also felt their various kinds of grief, although not as deeply as he. The wife, although admitting that she would miss the dog, had looked upon the sorrow of her family as unnecessary and insisted that there would be no more pets in her household. Bertocci allowed her to have her way, but in a few weeks began to feed any stray cat that came into the yard looking for food. One particular cat had in some way captured his affections. It was a small gray tabby with matted fur. When it came in from the fields where it would hunt and breed, he would take it upon himself to cut the burs out of its fur or clean its wounds. In the winter, if the weather turned excessively cold, he would give the animal shelter in the cellar and feed it until it again decided to leave. It was this cat that Domenick Sardo planned to capture, slaughter and dress, and present to Bertocci as the meat of a rabbit.

From his window now, with the shade pulled partly down so that he could look over the sill without being seen, Sardo began looking for the cat each day. Sometimes during the morning, before leaving for his shop, he would see it moving along the fence, jump into Bertocci's yard, walk up to the cellar door and wait. As usual Bertocci came out, picked the cat up tenderly in his arms and took it in. When Sardo saw this, his excitement increased. He would pace back and forth across the floor of his darkened room, rubbing his palms together rapidly, wondering with a heightened curiosity how he would capture the animal.

Finally, he decided to leave a dish of food on his own back steps. One morning he found the cat eating the food he had left out the night before. He picked the animal up, brought it into his house and locked it in a closet where it remained until he returned that night. When his son Angelo saw the cat, he gave it no more attention than he would have had it always been in the house. Sardo, relieved of having to explain the reasons for its presence, began considering how he would present the meat to Bertocci. He thought of an intermediary, but could think of no one he could trust. Next he thought of asking a stranger, but he was sure that Bertocci would ask the stranger where he had come across the meat. So with his plans incomplete, Domenick Sardo fed the cat, watched it closely and hoped for a solution.

By the end of the week, still unable to find a way to present his gift, the shoemaker became preoccupied with the possibility that his plan might not succeed. He found himself making mistakes in the stitching of leather soles and in the number of nails necessary to hold a heel firmly in place. When customers began bringing their shoes back for faulty work, he tried to show his mistakes were something that could have happened from the way the customers walked. Influenced by their opinions that it was the fault of his workmanship, he would take the shoes back and rework them in fits of heated anger. At home he began to brood in silence, sitting by the window of his room while the cat lay asleep on his bed. He watched moodily day after day as Bertocci, who feared that the cat had taken ill, began to move about the neighborhood in the hope of finding the animal.

One day, unable to stay put in his room, Sardo followed him to the fields and, hiding behind a rise of earth, listened to him call for the animal in tones filled with sorrow. He followed him unseen through the stalks of dry weeds, over the grassy mounds, along the gravel bed of the railroad tracks and back along the edge of the field to his house where, before going inside, he would sit on the back steps looking exhausted and forlorn. Each day now Bertocci would make his trek through the fields. Each day the shoemaker would follow behind. Then one night, after going to bed in a mood of deep confusion, Sardo had his first upsetting dream. He saw the cat in quartered pieces walking on the ceiling of his room. He saw the faces of his father and of the priests staring accusingly at him. Each night the clarity of the dream increased. During the day he felt himself overcome by a haunting lassitude. He began to eat less. He kept his shop closed for days at a time, and by the end of the month could not bring himself to leave his house.

One night he woke from his dream with a cry that went beyond the walls of his room. Tenants gathered in the hallway. Angelo, who had been out, returned just as the police considered breaking down the door. Hearing the piercing wails of his father, he opened the door and upon entering the apartment found his father standing on a chair in the kitchen with a rope around his neck, reaching for the light fixture above his head. When he saw the police, Sardo broke into a series of choking sobs. Coaxed down from the chair, the rope removed from his neck, he was taken in a state of mumbling hysteria to the city hospital under guard of the police. In the excitement, the cat walked out of the apartment, went down the hallway stairs and out into the yard.

From his window, Bertocci had seen the patrol car pull up in front of the shoemaker's house. Putting on his coat he went out and moved cautiously to the steps leading up into the doorway. He heard the commotion of voices and the pitiable moaning of Domenick Sardo coming from inside the hallway. When he saw the two policemen coming down the stairs holding the shoemaker by the arms, he looked with disbelief into the Sicilian's bony face. The shoemaker looked back at him with a dazed, hopeless stare, and as he was pulled toward the police car, he glanced at Bertocci over his shoulder as if to beg forgiveness; his mouth twisted painfully and his lips trembled in his attempt to speak. After the patrol car pulled away and the crowd that had stood about the front of the house began to leave, Bertocci, confused, shook his head and went home.

Bertocci felt no suspicion when he saw the cat run out of the shoemaker's house. But in a few days he began to feel an increasing sense of blame for his neighbor's predicament. He had merely to close his eyes now to see the hopeless expression in the shoemaker's eyes, and the quiver on his lips as he was pulled by the police toward the waiting patrol car. He wandered about the house with a detachment that bewildered the rest of the family. He thought of telling his wife how he felt but could not bring himself to do it. During the day she would find him staring blankly through the parlor window to the deserted street. At night she listened to his mumbling while he slept and in the morning could see the heavy stare in his eyes as if he had not slept at all. She said little to him, only that if he felt bad he should see the doctor. Bertocci would not answer her. He would simply shake his head from side to side, get up from his chair and begin pacing from room to room, his hands in the pockets of his coat sweater, his head lowered and his feet shuffling in their slippers on the wooden floor. At the kitchen table the family sat nervously, each as conscious of Bertocci's unhappiness as he was unaware of their knowledge of it. He only picked at the food that his wife began to leave for him on the kitchen table. One morning, she woke to find her husband gone.

When Bertocci had gotten out of bed that morning, he thought of telling his wife the reasons for his worries. He wanted to tell her of the hatred he had at times felt for Domenick Sardo. He wanted to tell her of the desire he had had to see Sardo suffer with the same indifference he had shown toward his wife while she suffered before her death. He wanted to tell her that if the shoemaker returned from the hospital in good health he would give him a present of five gallons of wine. But after thinking this over he instead decided on telling a certain priest in the parish, a Father Letino, whom he had come to know casually by way of his having baptized all of his children. It was this priest then, whom Bertocci, having wakened that morning filled with intense worry, had gone to see.

The church was located about a half mile from Bertocci's house. Holding his head down to avoid the stares of the neighbors who knew him, he made the trip in less than twenty minutes. When he reached the church, he stood looking up at the painted gold cross on the peak of the small steeple. The structure was a stucco-walled building whose stained-glass windows were framed by opened wooden beams. Leading up to the heavy wooden doors, with their bronze ring handles mounted on brass plates, and in which were carved the figures of all the saints in relief, were seven granite steps that stretched the full length of the church. On either side of the doors were two squat concrete urns whose plants, withered to sprigs now, stood naked against the background of gray stucco. Bertocci, looking at all of this, could not remember when he had last seen the church. He scratched in back of his ear. He drew his finger under his wet nose. He studied the figures on the door, enshrined forever it seemed in eternal flight. Slowly, a spasm started in his stomach. He took a short breath, scratched his ear again and with his thumb and forefinger worked the tip of his nose in quick little pulls. "It is senseless, I will not go in," he said in Italian, and suddenly the space between himself and the door of the church seemed to widen beyond his comprehension. He stood in the center of the sky, it seemed. He floated in the emptiness of the world. A trembling started in his legs. His mouth went dry. "Senseless," he tried to say again, but no sound came from his throat. He half turned himself away. He looked at the doors, at the urns, at the cross on the steeple. "Senseless," he finally said aloud, and turning

toward home, took no more than a step when the peal of
bells seemed to fall out of the sky itself, vibrating in his
head with the tremor of a struck anvil. He stopped and
turned his gaze up at the cross, which began to glow in the
morning light. He looked at the massive doors whose figures floated in the wood. He blinked his eyes and the
twigs in the urn were plush with thick green leaves, and
full red flowers burst among them. Ciro Bertocci, with his
nose dripping in the chill of the fall air, his woolen cap
pulled down over his lined forehead, stood dumbfounded
in his fear. *"Sacra rappresentazione,"* he said in a whisper
and his hand came up along his chest and blessed him in
the sign of the cross. "Are you all right?" he heard from
behind. Bertocci turned to the passer-by. *"Si,"* he said,
shaking his head rapidly. *"Si.* I am all right. I am all
right," and with this he turned from the church, looked
back once more and hurried home.

Once in his house Bertocci calmed himself by sitting
quietly in his chair in the parlor. He remained there
throughout the rest of the day. By the time the supper
meal was ready he had collected himself enough to eat
everything that was on his plate. That night while lying in
bed beside his wife he asked quietly if the church, in the
years he had not seen it, had changed. His wife knew
then he had that day made a visit. She told him that
nothing about the church had changed since the day
Robert was baptized, over twelve years ago. She described the granite steps, the carved wooden doors, the
urns that stood on each side of the doors, and the flowers
that grew in them during the summer. Then it came to
him: the church on the day of his son's baptism, the sunlight glowing on the cross, the plants in the urns plush
with red flowers and green leaves, and the bells pealing in
the warm air of that summer afternoon. With a sigh he
rolled over away from his wife.

"Allucinazione," he said sadly.

"Che cosa?" his wife asked.

"Niente," Bertocci answered and before falling to sleep he somehow came to realize that he would never see the Sicilian again.

part THREE

xii

Anthony continued to work at the arsenal after the wine had been sealed. He did not speak to his father about the permission forms until they were finally signed only four days before his birthday. The father had said little to him up to this point, but on the night the papers were signed, Bertocci wished before the whole family that his son would remain safe and would come home without wounds or scars. Anthony returned the papers to the recruiting officer the next day and was sworn into the navy. He was told that he would probably be called for boot camp within the next three days. As it was, he came home from work on the night of the second day, Wednesday, and found his father reading his orders which had arrived in the afternoon mail.

Before eating supper, Anthony read the orders himself. He was to report to the Norfolk Naval Training Base, Virginia, no later than twelve o'clock midnight, on Friday. He was to meet a recruiting officer from his district who would take him along with other recruits by rail to New York. From there, the order read, they would be taken by rail to Virginia. He was to take nothing with him except his shaving gear, a comb, a toothbrush, and the clothes that he wore. The order was signed by the same officer whose name had appeared on the approval papers.

Anthony put the orders down. His mother reached across the table and placed her hand on his. The two sisters and Robert looked on silently, and the father, leaning back in his chair with his arms folded, coughed lightly once, cleared his throat and spoke:

"It is the same name on the other papers? He is Italian. No?"

"Commander Compi," Anthony said. "Yes, it sounds Italian. Why?"

"If he is Italian he can help you maybe."

"I don't need help. Besides, he is not the commander of the whole navy. It's only this district."

"You have seen him?"

"I've never seen him. I don't even know who he is."

"Maybe if you can talk with him?"

"What for?" Anthony asked confusedly.

"They will need many sailors here."

"They'll need them everywhere."

"Maybe you can stay here if you can talk with him."

Anthony wiped his mouth with the back of his hand. "I don't want to stay here," he said. "And I'll go wherever I'm sent."

The father leaned back and unfolded his arms. "You talk without sense," he said.

"Please, Ciro," said the mother. "Tomorrow will be his

last night with us." With this she placed her hand on her son's and looked across at her husband.

Bertocci was gone most of the next day. He returned in the late afternoon with a package wrapped in brown paper tied securely with butcher's twine. When his wife asked him what he had bought, he smiled calmly, put the package into the ice chest and went into the cellar. In a few minutes he came back up carrying a hack saw, a mallet and a cold chisel, which he placed side by side on the kitchen table. He was in a happy mood. He went to the ice chest, removed his package and closed the door, carefully setting the bronze latch in place. With the package on the table now, and his wife and children standing off behind him with something of confusion and expectancy in the look on their quiet faces, he began to untie the butcher's twine. Under the first layer of paper was another of wax soaked through with blood where the creases had weakened it. As the family looked on and studied the unfamiliar shape of the object inside, Bertocci peeled the wax paper back and exposed the skinless head of a lamb. "It is for one who is honored," he said in Italian and with this he placed the head in one palm and held it up for all of them to see.

The wife was taken aback with surprise. The daughters sighed and looked away from the gleaming head with its layers of white gristle on the cheeks and its stained teeth fully visible on the long narrow jaw bones, and Robert, who moved up a little closer, was startled by the naked blue eyes bulging raw in their bony sockets. Bertocci's smile broadened. In English he said: "It is for you, Antonio, but first it must be cleaved."

Anthony smiled curiously as his father turned back to the table and put the head down.

"Antonio," he said. "You hold it like this and I will cut."

He held the head firmly between his two palms against the table.

"Come, *aspeto*," he said, and Anthony, after hesitating a moment, moved up beside his father, took hold of the head and held it in place as he was shown. Bertocci then with the mallet in one hand and the chisel in the other made his way to the other side of the table.

The wife turned to Robert and her daughters and asked them to leave the room, for it was in her mind to prevent an occurrence from which she had once before suffered a deep humiliation. It was some ten years ago after a distant relative on Bertocci's side had made an unexpected visit. Bertocci had not seen the man nor heard from him in twenty years. He was a short thin man with friendly eyes and a quiet nature, and when Bertocci asked him to sit and eat, he realized that his presence, although welcomed, could put a strain on the family's hospitality, since he could see they had just finished their evening meal minutes before his arrival. In honesty he explained that he himself had eaten a meal in the city a short while ago and there was no need to put out any food. But Bertocci insisted on his eating at least something and would not heed the man's desire for a simple glass of wine. The wine was put out, and along with it, a large flat plate of cheese, meat, oil-cured olives and a fresh loaf of Philomena Bertocci's bread. Feeling that this was not enough, Bertocci explained that later in the evening, when they could be alone, they would eat of a lamb's head together: a custom among some Italians, culminating in the guest's eating the eyes of the lamb as a gesture that showed his respect for the host. To this the relative had agreed, but said that he had to meet his train and could not stay beyond nine o'clock. The two men then, after their wine and some conversation about their common relatives in Italy, went out to buy the lamb's head.

It was the first one Philomena Bertocci had been asked

to cook. As a child she had seen several lambs' heads cooked by her own mother whenever a relative or an old friend of the family made a visit. Once, during such a visit, while sitting quietly at the table listening to the amenities of old friends, she saw her father remove the two eyes of the baked lamb's head and present them to the guest of honor. There had been much talk, she remembered, and when the eyes were offered the group fell into a jovial silence, stood up and toasted the honored guest with wine, while one by one he put the eyes into his mouth and chewed. The girl was filled with consternation then, and the father had allowed her to leave the room. Now Philomena Bertocci would cook a lamb's head for the guest who was in her household, and when the two men returned, she prepared it according to her husband's instructions. It had already been cleaved into halves by the butcher, and it was only a matter now of making slits into the various portions of the cheeks and tongue and stuffing the slits with garlic. Garlic too was placed between the skull wall and the brain. Olive oil was then wiped on and after seasoning, the two halves were put into the oven to bake. All of this Philomena did willingly, and later that night after the meal had been eaten and she was lying awake in her bed, she felt a consummate pride in what she had prepared.

But it was the humiliation she had suffered on the day following the relative's visit that brought on in her now the uncertainty of whether or not she would cook a lamb's head even for her son. For on that day, the garbage man, upon emptying her garbage into his truck, saw the meatless bones of the head which he mistook for the bones of a dog. She remembered that he wore a black rubber apron and had a round overhanging stomach, and that his derisive laugh carried into her household. Getting up from her chair she looked out into the street and saw that a small crowd had gathered at the rear of the garbage man's truck and stood looking at the bones. Realizing suddenly what it was they thought they saw, she ran out of the house into the street with a simple hope of explaining what the bones really were. She came up to the little group and began telling them of the relative's visit the night before, but when she saw the unbelieving expression that came into their stubborn faces and when they began turning away one by one without listening, she knew that her explanation was useless. She tried then to convince the garbage man, but he stood with his fists on his hips shaking his head from side to side, looking accusingly into her pained, hopeless face. With another derisive laugh he stepped into the cab of his truck and before driving off scowled at her through the window with disgust. Humiliation and rage had filled her then, and it was not long after this that much of the neighborhood held passionately to its belief that the family of Philomena Bertocci ate dogs.

Bertocci positioned the chisel at a point midway in back of the eyes and the center of the skull. He would first tap the chisel to make a guide channel for the blade of his hack saw. Then he would saw the head in two. The chisel was placed and the mallet was raised. Anthony closed his eyes and on the first tap of the mallet he could hear the bone give under the metal. A fissure a half-inch long was made. Into this Bertocci placed the blade of his hack saw and began a slow back and forth movement that in a short while cleaved the head in two. The halves were parted. Bertocci placed the hack saw down and wiped his forehead. He was happy.

The wife had watched all of this in silence. There was a look of uncertainty on her face as she went up to the table and stood with her hands on the edge. She studied the two halves with their exposed brains and the limp tongue attached to the lower jawbone of one half.

"I will not cook it," she said firmly.

Bertocci looked at her, said nothing and turned back to his lamb's head. With a cloth he wiped the table clean of bone gristle made from the blade of the saw, folded the cloth neatly and looked at her again.

"Is it without honor for your son that you refuse?" he asked.

In her southern Italian dialect she answered him. "It is because of my dignity that I refuse, for you have a mind that forgets what happened to me when the people here would not believe in the honor of your relative. Yes, you forget, Ciro Bertocci, that it was I who suffered to explain the bones of your feast, not you. And when I saw the people on the streets it was not honor that moved them to look at me as one who fed her family the meat of dogs." She paused and then added softly: "I say I will not cook it."

Bertocci smiled, and imitating her accent slightly, said, "It is not honor for your son then. It is for yourself that you refuse. So I will cook it, and you will have your dignity."

"Do as you will," Philomena Bertocci said, raising her voice, "but the bones will not be put out by me. You will take them away and bury them." With this she left her kitchen, while her husband, tantalized by his little victory, prepared the head for baking.

Once the halves of the lamb's head were in the oven Bertocci went into the bedroom. He returned with his sweater, and while putting his arm through one of the sleeves said, "When you are to eat you will call for me." He finished buttoning his sweater and after the kitchen door closed behind him, they listened to his footsteps shuffling down the wooden stairs into the cellar.

The table was set and a portion of the steaming food was brought to it from the stove. Roberto was then asked to call for his father. At first he refused, but when his mother threatened to punish him, he went down into the cellar and found his father sitting on his stool before the wine barrels. Robert moved quietly up to the open door. He got just to the slant of light coming out of the little wine cellar and saw his father reaching down towards the bottom of one barrel. In a moment he heard the steady gurgle of wine flowing out of the spigot into the hollow of the tin cup. After the cup was full, he watched his father empty it carefully into a green quart bottle that he held between his legs. In a short while the bottle was full and he watched again as his father filled another.

With the two bottles side by side between his legs, Bertocci filled the cup again. He brought it up to his mouth and his head tipped farther and farther back under the yellow light of the bulb until the cup was empty. Robert came up closer as the father, mumbling something in Italian the boy could not understand, filled the cup again. He drank from it slowly, sipping from time to time, and the boy listened to the slurping of his lips against the tin.

Bertocci drank four more cups of wine. When he put the cup down on top of the barrel, he weaved sideways, quickly got his balance and saw his son standing in the frame of the open door. He leaned down and, without taking his eyes off Robert, picked up the two bottles of wine.

"Here, take this," he said. He held out one of the bottles by its neck.

Robert drew himself back. "We're going to have the supper now," he said hesitantly.

"Yes, take it for supper," the father answered.

"I will spill it," the boy said shyly.

The father moved the bottle in front of his son's face. "It will not spill. Take it," he said.

The boy reached out slowly with both of his hands and took hold of the bottle. "I will spill it," he said again.

"I say to you it will not spill. Come!"

With this the father moved through the doorway of his wine cellar. The boy, frightened, stepped to one side as he passed, looked up into his face and followed him as he stumbled across the floor to the stairs.

When his father made the turn onto the first step, the boy could just make out the small square of his back bent forward in the feeble light coming from the wine cellar. He watched him lift slowly to make his way up into the deeper shadows of the stairway. Holding the bottle tightly with both hands, he pulled it in closer to his chest and moved onto the steps behind. In the darkness now he became uncomfortable. He listened, with an apprehension he could not yet call fear, to the stringer beams of pine wheeze under their shifting weight like boughs in a wind, listened to their shuffling footsteps knock and scrape as they stepped onto each loose board of the stairs. By the time they got halfway up, he felt a trembling start in his legs and his hands shook, causing gouts of wine to spill out of the bottle onto his chest. Quickly, with his heartbeat seemingly audible, he covered the top of the open bottle with one hand. But as they moved further up on the narrow stairway the trembling in his legs ceased and his hands became steady round the top of the bottle. It was then that he realized that his fear was not the fear of spilling wine, or the fear of the dark; but he could still hear the beating of his heart. And while he watched the baggy trouser legs of his father barely visible in front of him, and heard the sudden rasps of his father's tired breathing when he braced himself against the wall to rest, he knew with an acute sense of shame that it was the closeness to his father in the dark that made him feel afraid. And because he could see no head somewhere above the black shape in front of him—a shape that weaved erratically as it did against the wall on its way up the landing— he imagined his father headless.

In preparation for the supper, the kitchen table had

been moved away from the window to the middle of the floor. And because the mother had asked for more light, two one-hundred-watt bulbs had been bought at the corner store. They were now used to replace the smaller ones that had hung from the ceiling in a frosted globe. While Anthony screwed the new bulbs into the sockets, his mother washed the globe clean and wiped it dry. This done, she handed it up to Anthony, who was standing on a chair. He placed the globe carefully into position and tightened the small screws that held it to the fixture. When the switch was thrown, the new light, compared to the yellowish glow from the previous bulbs, evenly dissolved the shadows which always seemed to have darkened the steaming kitchen. Now they could see clearly the shape and the details of every object, where before they were only slightly visible.

Anthony had just gotten down from the chair when the kitchen door opened and the father stepped in with the bottle of wine in his hand. Behind the father Robert stood quietly, still holding his bottle hard against his chest. After a moment, he walked past his father to the table, placed the bottle on top and with his fingers wiped off the few drops of wine that beaded down its neck. Bertocci, too, walked to the table, squinted in the glare of the kitchen and looked up into the brilliance of the globe burning white above his head. He put the bottle down and focused his eyes upon the gleaming black Glenwood stove, with its cluster of aluminum pots—two of which were yet steaming, and the steam wraithing above the stove, whiter now than he had ever seen it. Then he looked at the pulsing glare of the white linen curtains. Where the curtains parted, he could see the glistening texture of steam clouding on the glass of the windows. With his eyes squinting, he turned his head and stared up into the miniature sun exploding white above his head. Without anyone speaking, they watched him patiently as he scanned, with his face up and his mouth opened loosely, the desolate expanse of the white plaster ceiling. His eyes followed the grainy patterns of filler that mapped the lines of the hidden cracks beneath it, and coursed slowly along the edge to the corner where the ceiling joined the glaring buff color of the walls. Turning toward the center of the ceiling he concentrated his stare upon the glowing, ball-like protuberance of glass through which he could see the source of white fire exploding in his eyes.

Bertocci lowered his head, reached out and held the edge of the table and closed his eyes. He swayed to one side. Anthony took hold of his arm and tried to steady him while the wife, in her attempt to help, tipped over a chair. She set the chair upright and pushed it into the back of his knees. Bertocci opened his eyes. When he felt the chair against his legs he turned around, looked blankly into the face of his wife, and sat himself down.

"It is all right," he said. "It is only that there is much light here." He looked into Anthony's face now. "I have wine for his supper. He will drink it."

"Yes, Ciro," his wife said. "We will eat first. *Aspetto.*"

He turned to his son. "It is the wine of his labor I have drunk."

Anthony looked at the two bottles. "You weren't going to open it."

"It is the wine for your supper," the father said. He took hold of one of the bottles. "We will drink of it now, Antonio."

"Please, Ciro. When we eat. It is ready," the mother said.

Bertocci raised his voice. "Before there is anything we eat. We will drink of it now." He filled a glass and handed it to his son. "Take; drink, Antonio. This is your labor." Anthony took the glass while his father filled another for himself.

"Is it what you wanted?" Anthony asked, staring into the glass.

"It is a good zinfandel," said the father. "It has in it the blood of your labor." He held the glass up to the light.

"*Aspetto,* Ciro," the mother broke in. "We should eat the supper now."

"We will drink now," Bertocci said slowly.

"Maybe we should wait," Anthony said. "You've had . . ."

"We will drink," the father said. He raised the glass of wine, his hand shaking, and he held it up before them in the light. "Take; drink, Antonio," he went on. "It is the juice of your labor. I say to you I will not drink of it again until it is here that you will return." There was a silence between them. Anthony then lifted his glass, and as his father began to drink, he too brought the wine to his lips and they both drank until their glasses were empty.

After the first course of the supper was eaten, Bertocci became set on eating the lamb's head with his son. He got up and took the halves from on top of the stove; still warm, they were placed in a large platter side by side. Standing above his family he asked that a place be cleared for the platter, and when this was done, he set the lamb's head down in the center of the table.

He said in Italian, "It is for you, Antonio, that we will eat of these. And the eyes, because they are for one who is honored, will be yours to eat at this table in this house."

While the family looked on in silence Bertocci removed the meat from the halves and spooned out the brains. The meat and brains were then put into two saucers, one of which he put in front of Anthony and the other in front of himself. Pulling up his chair now, he sat down at the table and ate the first piece of lamb. A smile came to his lips as he chewed. He looked at his elder son.

"You will eat of it now," he said.

Anthony raised his fork and took a small sliver of meat from the saucer. When he finished the first piece he ate the rest and sat looking at the small cooked brain that remained. "I don't want it," he said. "And I don't know if I can eat the eyes."

"The brain is not necessary," Bertocci said. "But the eyes, yes." Then, as if removing the core of an apple he detached the eyes from their sockets with a paring knife, put them into two different saucers, and again placed one saucer in front of his son and the other in front of himself. Anthony stared at the cloudy blue sphere with its gleaming white nerve tissue and the round bulk of fat attached to the rear of the eyeball itself.

"I can't," he said softly. "I can't eat it."

"I will eat the first, then," Bertocci said. He picked up the eye with his fingers, looked at it a moment and put it into his mouth. Smiling, he began to chew, and after a while the smile left his face and the memory of all he had eaten in honor of relatives and friends came over him; and now it was his son that he was honoring, and in his revery the son too and all that his son meant to him came to him. And as he chewed he felt that his family were all suddenly strangers, sitting at his table and in his house, for he had eaten the first alone. He looked now at the faces of his wife and children, all of whom sat quietly watching him, and he knew he could not force upon them his wish to honor his elder son. So he put the other eye into his mouth, and as slowly and as carefully as he had eaten the first, he chewed until this one too was eaten. And he did so without resentment for his son.

During the remainder of the supper Bertocci said little. He had filled all of the glasses with wine and was himself drinking from the second bottle which was almost empty. His wife, who was intermittently in and out of her chair going from the stove to the table with the hot food, had not drunk any of the wine. Bertocci began to wonder about this, and while she sat at the table in silence, he watched her ignore her children whenever one of them sipped the wine from his glass. His head cleared for a time after he had eaten a small portion of spaghetti and a piece of stuffed meat, but now as he stared at his wife his eyes became heavy-lidded and his head nodded lower over his plate. He pulled his head up and looked across at his wife again. That his son would not eat of the lamb's eyes he could understand, though with solemnity; but his wife's refusal to drink of the wine he had labored for was unforgivable.

"You will drink before the supper is done," he said loudly. Then in Italian and emphatically he said, "It is of your son."

His wife put down her fork and swallowed. She looked into his eyes. "Because of that," she said, "I will not drink with you!"

"It is of him," Bertocci said.

"It is of you," his wife said in Italian, "and it is because of you I will not drink."

Bertocci was silent. He reached for the bottle and filled the glass again. He drank the wine and pushed himself on his chair away from the table. Then with his hand on the edge, he raised himself up from his chair and stood looking down at his family. He swayed to one side, braced himself and, in Italian, said, "It is better that you will finish this supper alone." He hesitated, then he added slowly, "It is better you will not be offended by me this night."

He left the table and stumbled across the floor into his room to sleep.

By the time Bertocci woke the next morning Anthony had already said goodbye to Robert, his two sisters, and his mother, who had stayed awake most of the night kneeling on a pillow before the lighted statue praying. During the commotion before Anthony left the house, the sisters broke into prolonged sobbing. The mother too cried spasmodically, and had forgotten about her husband. Anthony left then without having said goodbye to his father. When Bertocci woke up and learned that his son was gone, he swore aloud and yelled in Italian that his wife had deliberately let him sleep and that he was certain now that she must be something more than a fool. He got out of bed, and without dressing, sat at the kitchen table in his underwear drinking the wine left over from supper.

After his daughters had left for work and Robert had gone off to school, he went into the cellar to find a shovel. Bertocci stood quietly in the frame of the open cellar door musing on the dustlike covering of snow that had fallen during the night. One hand tightened around the shovel's handle, the other around the neck of the wrinkled paper bag in which were the bones of the lamb. In front of him across the space of the yard the leafless elm swayed in the silence of dying wind: the thick bare angular limbs of the elm swayed noiselessly from the pivot of its huge trunk into the complexities of its upper branches. Bertocci looked up into the network of branches. He listened to the absence of sound in the movement. Beyond the tree the sun diffused its light through a layer of clouds and mist.

"It will snow again," he thought. He lowered his head and listened to the silence. He thought of the day they had unloaded the grapes and stacked the boxes in the shade of the tree. He thought of the Negro, of the dealers, of the wagon, of the horse, and of the grapes crushing cool in the barrels and the wine they had made. Presently he thought of a time before the grapes and the wine, before his time alone on Ellis Island among the faces he had never come to know. He thought of the town in Italy where he was born, of the first desire to leave that had welled up in him with promise, that welled up in him even now, like the passing of a dream. And he thought of his father, and of his mother and of the sorrow in the lines of her face. Of his sisters, too, he thought, and of his relatives, most of them dead now—for how many years he did not know—who had gathered in the shade of the grove with the tables laden with food and the wine pouring cool from the big wooden keg in the shade of the trees, and of the blessings they had given him before he left. "All so long ago," he said in Italian. And now of his son Antonio he thought, and he looked up at the tree again, stilled by the absence of wind in the cold light. And all these things he thought about caused him no sorrow. A longing came over him, and he lowered his head and stepped out of the frame of the cellar door and moved over the frozen earth of the yard toward a clearing in the snow at the base of the tree: a stubble of dead grass beneath the base of the tree where he would bury the bones of the lamb.

xiii

When he came back into the house, Bertocci knew by the weakness in his legs that he was going to be drunk again. He made his way to the bedroom, staggered through the door, and fell onto the bed beside his wife, who had fallen to sleep disgusted. Now she woke and turned away from him. He started to mumble incoherently, lying outside of the covers with his eyes closed. Before she fell off to sleep again she listened to sounds of his coughing and to the sudden, heavy gasping for air. She became frightened. She blessed herself and her fear diminished. She closed her eyes, and slowly brought one hand up from under the bedclothes and covered her ear.

Bertocci's wife woke at noontime and found him gone. She got out of bed, did what little work had to be done in her kitchen, and waited for her husband to come up from the cellar where she was sure he was drinking more of the wine. She waited until late afternoon. When he did not come up, she went down and found him sitting drunk on his stool, asleep against the wall. His chin lay upon his chest. His head leaned to one side on his shoulder. His legs were outstretched in front of the barrels, and there was an overturned gallon between them. The wine had flowed out of the jug and had stained the floor like blood. The sleeves of his sweater and of the flannel shirt that he wore beneath it were rolled up to the elbows. Streaks of dried wine were caked in the hair of his bare arms, which hung loosely at his side.

His wife tried to wake him. She shook him by the shoulders. She slapped him lightly on the face. He grunted, brought his hand up instinctively to protect himself, and struck her on the chin. She fell backwards through the door as Bertocci, losing his balance, slipped along the wall and fell full against the barrels. She came back into the wine cellar, her chin numb from the blow, and angrily straightened her husband on the stool. His head fell against the wall. Then with both hands, she grabbed him by the shoulders and shook him repeatedly, swearing in Italian an accursed denunciation into his drunken face.

Three weeks passed before the letter came from Anthony. It was addressed to his mother, but because she could not read she asked Robert to read it aloud to all of them. In the letter Anthony said that his training was hard and began in the morning when it was still dark. It went on all day and ended sometimes as late as twelve o'clock at night. Because of this, he said, he was always tired and spent most of his time off in bed. He had tried to write letters six or seven times before but he was never satisfied with what he wrote and so he tore them up. He closed by saying he was sorry he had not said goodbye to his father, and that he did not know when he would write again.

During the next four weeks, while they waited for a letter, Philomena and her two daughters increased their visits to church. Robert, too, attended mass every morning before going to school. At home sometimes during the day, and before going to bed at night, the wife would pray in Italian at the foot of the statue, while her husband, watching from the bed, mocked her under his breath.

Bertocci's refusal to believe in prayer became stronger. He had refused to pray even on the first Christmas Eve after Anthony's departure. On that night, a night held sacred by the family, he denounced the church vindictively and swore hatefully against their God. In her irritation and fear, his wife left him alone in the house, and with her family, fled to the midnight mass to pray. When they returned home they found him drunk at the kitchen table. The gallon jug of wine was three-quarters empty in front of him.

This was the first prolonged drinking he had done since Anthony had left for the navy. He had bought twenty-five new one-gallon jugs at an auction and had filled them with wine. After he gave two of them to the neighbor and two to his cousin, as he had promised, he lined them against the walls of the wine cellar. He had made up his mind then not to drink any more wine either from the barrels or from the gallon jugs. But his refusal to drink had lasted only until Christmas and he now drank almost a gallon and a half of wine each day.

Bertocci ate little, and when he did eat, it was always in silence. He would sit morosely at the table, his gallon of wine on the floor beside his leg. He would drink himself into misery until he fell off to sleep in his chair. He never spoke about Anthony nor did he read any of the letters that came. The Zenith was never turned on and the newspapers were left unread on the kitchen table. Whenever his family talked about the war or about his son's involvement in it, he would leave for the cellar or for his room. He drank throughout the day and went to bed drunk at night. His wife, who became tolerant only because his tirades had lessened, was worried now over his refusal to eat. He grew thinner, and when he coughed he came near to suffocation.

One night in late January, after an attack of prolonged, spasmodic coughing, he forbade them to call for a doctor, and when the attack subsided, he threatened to leave the household for good if anyone so much as mentioned his illness. Finally, his wife's only wish was that he keep himself warm in the dampness of his wine cellar. He could do this for his own good, she said, by putting on warmer clothing. Bertocci scorned her concern.

They did not hear from Anthony until the middle of the second week in January. The mother gave the letter to Robert to read aloud at table. In it Anthony said he had gone to California. From there he had been shipped out to a group of islands in the Pacific called the Admiralties. He lived on one of them, Manus, with about five hundred other sailors. Their job, he said, was to supervise the loading and unloading of vessels that came into the port. The Japanese attacked the base once in a while from the hills, but he felt he was safe and there was no need to worry about him. It was very hot most of the time. He closed by saying that he had not worn a navy uniform since he got there. He wore only dungarees. Much of what he had said was censored, but they now knew where he was and because of this they were relieved. Bertocci had not read the letter.

A week later another letter came, in which Anthony said he had been transferred. His duty now was helping to bulldoze holes in the ground. "Into these holes," he said, "we plow the bodies of dead Japanese soldiers who have been killed in raids. Once in the holes their bodies are soaked with gasoline and burned. Then they are covered over." Robert faltered while he read. Anthony had stopped writing abruptly on the last word and signed his name. Bertocci, who had been listening from the bedroom where he was lying down, got up and went into the cellar. His wife, his two daughters and Robert went to church to pray.

Another letter came a week later. In it Anthony told them that he, along with some other sailors—the number was censored—had been assigned to an undermanned army company that had been fighting in the area. He said this transfer was unusual, but that all the available men on the island were needed to fight the Japanese, who were attacking from the hills continually day and night in their final attempt to destroy the base. The next day still another letter came which, because it was almost completely censored, seemed meaningless to the family. Only two hours after they had tried to read it the mother received a telegram from the Department of the Navy, stating that her son Anthony had died in the service of his country on February 10 from gun wounds inflicted upon himself.

Bertocci had been in the cellar most of the afternoon. He came up when he heard the sudden wailing coming from the kitchen. He had not shaved for almost five days. The flesh under his eyes reflected a wan pallor against the dark, gray stubble of his beard. Although he had not been drinking, he still looked dishevelled, with his baggy woolen pants drooping from his waist and his sweater, buttoned unevenly in the front, hanging loosely from his narrow shoulders. He stood like a shadow in the kitchen doorway. He said nothing. He showed no surprise when he saw his wife crying and his two daughters holding each other, moaning beside her. He shuffled across the threshold to the table. He saw the opened telegram envelope on the tablecloth, and then the telegraph itself clutched in the fist of his wife's hand. He knew that his son was dead.

He said nothing to them, nor did their crying lessen when they looked up and saw him standing above them. Quietly, he turned back to the door, shook his head, and made his way down into the wine cellar.

He remained in the cellar for a long time, sitting before the two barrels silently, staring at the gallon jugs of wine lined against the wall. Now and then he would reach out slowly and rub his palm down along the staves of the barrel. Above him, from the kitchen, he could still hear the outbursts of crying and the hoarse quiver in the voice of his wife as she now bewailed over and over again in Italian the name of the blessed virgin. He brought his hand up to bless himself, hesitated, and let it fall back upon his knee. There was a tightening in his throat. He looked up at the bulb, and after a while, with his eyes watery and closed hard against the glare, he spoke the name of his son. But there was no sound and he could feel the word swell in his throat. He tried again. There was nothing. He brought his hands to his face and heard the name repeat itself like an echo within his brain. He opened his mouth and his lips began to move under his hands. Still there was nothing.

During the days that followed, Bertocci had not once talked to his wife about Anthony's death. She made no indication that she cared whether he did or not. She and her two daughters had gone immediately into mourning and saw little of him. They dressed in black now wherever they went, and spent many hours in church. The sisters had added black veils to their dresses. Bertocci refused to wear the arm band his wife had made out of black silk. When their few relatives came to pay their respects dressed in black, he fled to the cellar and remained there drinking until they left.

Like the rest of his family, he felt the unreality of Anthony's death. They had felt it more acutely when the last letter he had written reached them two weeks after his death. Bertocci refused to stay in the room while it was read. Later, he saw the letter on the bureau and took it with him into the cellar where he read it alone. He had difficulty in understanding the handwriting. He felt he was reading the words of a stranger. Over two-thirds of the letter was censored, but by the time he finished reading, he had understood enough to realize, at least for himself, the full import of his son's death. It came to him suddenly as a real and self-deprecating fact. He laid the letter down on top of the barrel, and felt the guilt of a man who, having dreamed he has killed, wakes to remain obsessed by his crime.

His body grew weaker. Seldom did he eat at table. He would instead take bits of food into the cellar. He would eat and spend the rest of the day silent on his stool, drinking before the wine barrels.

One day a registered letter came from the Department of the Navy. It explained that Anthony's property had been processed and would be sent home. When the footlocker and a box containing property of next of kin did arrive, Bertocci, with Robert's help, carried the locker into the wine cellar, where it was placed before the two barrels of wine. The key for its padlock was found in the box with Anthony's valuables. Bertocci never used it. That afternoon he drank heavily, and by nightfall he went into a stupor that kept him in bed almost unconscious for the next two days. He got up on the third day and learned from his wife that Angelo Sardo, who had been wounded seriously, had recovered and was coming home safe for good. When Bertocci heard this he dressed and went into the cellar to drink.

He would have remained in the cellar, but his wife, who had become concerned over his failing health, went down to get him after she heard the forecast of an oncoming storm. The temperature had already fallen to near freezing. The winds had increased to gusts, blowing hard against the house and shaking the windows in their frames. She found her husband sleeping with his head lying on the footlocker. By the time she got him awake and persuaded him to come up into the warmth of the kitchen, the snowing had started and the house shook under the force of the wind. She tried to get him into bed as Robert and his two sisters stood by, frightened. She held him by the shoulders and together they stumbled into the bedroom where he threatened to beat her. Then, drunkenly, he swore in Italian, cursing the black clothes they wore and the God they prayed to. The sisters and Robert cried loudly as Bertocci fell against his wife with his fists. Robert ran into the room and threw his arms around his father's legs, in an attempt to pull him away. He heard the fist above his head. He heard his mother's scream as she slid down against the wall to the floor. Bertocci, breathing heavily, fell drunk onto the bed, exhausted. They were all crying now, and the sisters blessed themselves hysterically. The wife, whose crying ceased, picked herself up from the floor and covered her husband who had fallen to sleep above the bedclothes. The she turned to her children, blessed herself and said because of the storm, they would pray for him at home.

They prayed a long time for Bertocci. When he woke

up it was morning, and he got out of bed to find his wife and daughters gone. His son told him they were at church. Bertocci said nothing. He dressed himself slowly by the window and looked out into the yard at the drifts of snow. Robert stood in the doorway and watched silently. Now and then Bertocci coughed spasmodically and his face reddened. He got his sweater on and looked again out into the yard. His eyes traced the laden branches of the elm and followed along its trunk to where the snow had drifted in a swirl around its base. He stared solemnly at the base, at the contours of the drift above the ground where he had buried the bones of the lamb. He looked across the yard to the fence and to the frozen tips of the pickets. There was a bare patch of earth and stubbled grass where the drifts had not taken; and along the fence again to where it reached the garden, he could see the tops of the tomato stakes above the snow. Beyond the fence and the yard he could see the shoemaker's house standing out of the drifts, its windows partly visible through a sheet of white. He began to cough heavily, and when he stopped, he brought his hand shaking to his mouth and wiped it with the back of his hand. He looked once more out into the snow. "It is too clean," he said in Italian, and went down into the cellar to drink.

xiv

The boy thought about it for almost an hour. He paced from the bedroom to the kitchen, leaning for a while each time on the inside sill of the bedroom window and looking nervously at the snow outside. When he thought about it, he could hear it as though it were happening for the first time, with the same illogical suddenness. The idea

of it, which he tried to force out of his mind by talking
aloud to himself about the things he thought he could see
in the snow, produced in him the same terror that had
caused him to drive his nails into the thighs of his father's
legs. He could hear the fist now somewhere above his
ears, hitting into his mother's face, and he closed his eyes
and saw her slipping down against the wall. And while he
thought of it, standing by the window, he could feel again,
as he had then, the same texture of muscle in his father's
leg when his fingers had clawed like spikes through the
coarse fiber of his pants. And now he thought he would
cry. But he knew he would somehow do it, or he would at
least try. Resolutely, he held back the tightness in his
throat.

From the stairs the boy could see the open door of the
wine cellar and could hear his father's breathing. It was a
sound out of all proportion to the size and frailty of his
body. But while Robert stood there, the breathing
quieted and the father began to sleep. The boy mused on
what he saw and smelled as something inscrutable, yet it
held for him a sensate mystery: the two rotund oak barrels
standing squat against the granite stones of the wall; the
odor of dank grape husks and the smell of the pinewood
sawdust, sweet and heathery rising from the earthen floor
of the cellar; and his father, whose consciousness was
slaked away by the wine—motionless, save for the slow
heave of his back while he breathed, and silent now in his
brief reprieve from memory. His head shone partly bald
under the bulb hanging from the overhead beam, and the
tufts of hair at his temples looked like flakes of snow. The
boy left the shadows of the stairway and moved across the
open space until he stood just out of the light falling
through the open door of the wine cellar. He could now
see the splotched residue of wine against the white block
lettering of his brother's name on the footlocker; and he

could see a broken drinking glass, the seven or more empty gallon jugs along the base of the wall with rings of leftover wine settled on their insides. And above the footlocker he saw a framed picture of Christ with his heart exposed; the frame was made of cardboard, and through the film of dust on the little square of glass that it held, the halo was slightly visible. Below this, nailed to the wall, he saw the glossy snapshot of his brother. He was in uniform and his picture was fingerstained with wine.

As he looked, the sabbath bells rang from the steeple of the church and the throng moved up the brick steps that had been cleared of snow. Some people stood in small groups on the sidewalk, and when the bells had ceased they too walked up the steps and into the church, and the street and the sidewalk were deserted.

And the bells began to ring once more across the windless morning before the mass began, and the boy listened to them and he watched and the father woke up and spoke mournfully in Italian while he reached for the cup of wine on the footlocker, took it in his hand, and raised it to his mouth.

And the two hulking sisters, wrapped in their black shawls and wearing their black cloth hats, and the mother with her black coat still on and the black silk kerchief over her head were already in the church sitting among the parishioners. Some glanced at her before sidling into their pews, while others moved slowly down the aisle until all the pews were filled and the church was silent.

And the boy watched from the shadows and his father spoke again in Italian and raised his head back to receive the wine, and in his face was the same quality of hopeless despair that had been in his voice.

And the mother kneeled on one knee to balance herself and she blessed herself and whispered the trinity. And then she closed her eyes and put her face into her opened hands, and the black beads of her rosary hung from her fingers. And her daughters kneeled beside her and they, too, lowered their heads, and the mother lifted her head out of her hands and raised the rosary to her lips.

And the boy watched and felt again, as he had felt on the night he had run away, the same fear of a mystery whose reason he could not think into words; and it was because his father, who now began to weep behind the boarded walls of his wine cellar, his head lowered by self-pity and the memory of his elder son, was a different kind of man, different in his method of sorrow and so remote from the boy's own world of understanding that he was hardly a man at all. To hate him now would be like killing a stranger merely because he was strange.

And now the sisters closed their eyes and put their faces into their hands and their lips began to move in the mystery of their prayers. And the priest came out of the sacristy and kneeled to cross himself before the altar, and they all saw this and the sisters saw this and blessed themselves, and the mother too saw this and she blessed herself. And after a time they watched him raise the chalice to his lips and drink.

And the boy watched and the father drank until the cup was empty, and he placed it down on the footlocker and began filling it again from the gallon jug; and while he poured, his hands shook under the weight of the jug and he coughed heavily as the wine pulsed out of it. The father continued to pour until the cup was filled once more and the wine flowed over it; and he coughed again painfully, and his breath came quicker now; but he waited and then he passed his trembling hand through the ribbon of wine which flowed red on the footlocker and over the stenciled name of his son.

And they moved down the aisle to the rail before the altar, and she kneeled at the rail and she lifted up her face and with her eyes closed she received the host.

And the boy watched this silently from the shadows,

and his father coughed again and it was a sudden cough this time as if it had snapped something loose from within his chest; and the boy trembled when he heard it, and he closed his eyes, but the fear passed and in the silence that followed he was no longer afraid and he moved out of the shadows closer to the door and watched.